RULES
FOR THE
DEAD

CHRIS MCDONALD

ERIKA PIPER BOOK 3

Alison
You killed the
saint in me

RED DOG
UK

Published by RED DOG PRESS 2021

First Edition

Hardback ISBN 978-1-913331-39-9

Paperback ISBN 978-1-913331-25-2

Ebook ISBN 978-1-913331-26-9

www.reddogpress.co.uk

In memory of Sue Williams, who read *A Wash of Black* and convinced me it was good enough to be published.

We're all suckers for tragedy

1

AMANDA MAYHEM'S BODY lies on the floor beside the bed. Her eyes are closed and her long, tanned legs stretch out from below a flowery silk dressing gown. Clutched in her hand is a single lavender rose, the purple matching the colour of her perfectly manicured nails. She looks peaceful. On the immaculately made bed sits her husband, Johnny.

He has just murdered her.

His dark floppy hair falls over his eyes and course stubble darkens his jaw. His head is in his hands and when he looks up to see who has just come in to the bedroom, his shimmering emerald eyes are wet.

'Pause it, will you love?' asks Tom, as our son's cries from upstairs cut through the noise from the television. He pushes himself off the sofa and leaves the room, as I fumble down the side of the cushion for the remote control. I freeze the screen and laugh aloud at what it shows.

It's me.

Or rather, the actress who has been chosen to play me. The Erika Piper of this true crime drama.

Her high cheekbones, bagless eyes and perfectly pressed trouser suit flatter me, and are a far cry from what I remember looking like on that night, seven years ago. As Leo's cries are sated by a shushing Tom upstairs, I time travel back to that night in my head.

I remember walking through the unlocked door of the house Johnny and Amanda shared in Ashton-under-Lyne, a market town to the east of Manchester city centre. In the 90s, Johnny had ridden the Britpop wave and enjoyed success as the singer of The Darling Roses. Of the various horticulturally named bands, The Stone Roses had obviously gone on to headier heights, but Johnny's band's successes had afforded him a five-bed house in a sought-after area of the city. It had also brought him into the orbit of Amanda Paige; a model from the city who was making waves of her own.

As Kurt and Courtney's flame burned out on the other side of the Atlantic, Johnny and Amanda's was only beginning to smoulder; flickering, toying with combustion. And combust it did. The two became lovers. It would prove to be a volatile romance. This generation's Sid and Nancy. The red top papers loved them—the constant swapping of love for hate and back again was the gutter press's dream. When they arrived at a club or at a restaurant for a romantic celebration, cameramen were waiting, falling over each other to get the best angle. Much to the ire of Johnny who frequently lashed out, unable to stop himself rising to the bait constantly dangled in front of him.

When they announced they were getting married, articles questioned how wise that decision was and armchair experts speculated how long it would last.

The Darling Roses split up at the turn of the century, having made their money. Johnny and Amanda would probably never have to work another day in their lives. And, it seemed they'd defied all those who said their relationship was doomed to fail.

Until that night, seven years ago, when their relationship juddered to a halt in the most extreme way possible.

The front door had opened onto an expansive hallway flooded with light from LED spotlights embedded in the ceiling. Police officers made their way down the hall towards the rooms on the ground floor, their feet slapping on the tiled flooring. DI Simon Black and I stood in the entranceway, waiting, and after a fruitless search the officers assembled once more in the hall, eyeing the stairs. They led the way, climbing past framed album covers and live shots of Johnny whipping a crowded arena into a frenzy.

When we got to the top of the stairs, it was obvious where Johnny was. Visceral, animal-like howls came from the bedroom at the end of the landing. The door was slightly ajar. One of the officers assumed the lead and made his way cautiously along the strip of landing. I remember his heavy boots sinking into the plush carpet and thinking how out of place he looked. How out of place we all were.

When he got to the door, he took a breath to steady his nerves and shoved it open. He stepped back to reveal the scene.

Inside the bedroom, Johnny was sitting on the bed, though nothing about him was as cherubic as the dramatisation on television had depicted him. A filthy, dishevelled beard bunched around his shrieking mouth and lank, greasy hair hung over his bloodshot eyes. Eyes that popped with rage and dilated pupils that showed he was under the influence of some sort of illegal substance. In his hand, he casually twirled a blood-soaked baseball bat.

On the floor, at his feet, lay his wife. Unlike the television program's pre-watershed version, it did not look like she'd met a peaceful end. Lying on her front, her fair hair was matted with blood. A gash, presumably from the baseball bat, had opened up on the back of her head and was spilling blood onto the expensive cream carpet. Her lacy ivory lingerie was stained crimson. Blood splattered the walls and most of the furniture. It looked like one blow from the bat was all it took to end her life. A few more to make damn sure of it. There was one thing the program did get right though; a lavender rose had been placed in one of Amanda's hands.

Johnny had been handcuffed and led away. He had put up no resistance, but, as he was taken out of the room and down the stairs towards a waiting police car, he kept screaming that he'd been set up. DI Simon Black had congratulated the officers still in the room, unmoved by Johnny's vehement protestations. I remember feeling torn. There was something in Johnny's screams that got to me.

In the here and now, the living room door opens and Tom finally emerges from the hallway, retaking his place beside me on the sofa.

'Little Leo just needed a cuddle,' he says.

He looks at me; at my bitten nails and my furrowed brow and I can see that he is wondering whether or not to ask the question I've been asking myself. In the end, he does.

'Are you sure you want to watch this?'

I've contemplated this since the adverts first aired a month ago. Seeing Johnny's face did something to me. I've been tense, jumpy. That old cliché that every police officer has a case that sticks with them—this is mine.

I nod. I need to see it. Tom grabs the remote and presses play.

'Jesus, is that who they've chosen to play you?' he laughs, breaking the tension in the room as 'I' make my way around Amanda's body on screen. 'Who did you blackmail to get her as Erika Piper?'

I yank a hair from his chest and he grimaces. As I make my move for another, he calls for a truce and we both laugh.

On the screen, the recreation of the crime scene fades to black. It's been badly edited. The black is replaced with a cramped room. The walls are off-white. I suspect at some time in the past they were pristine, though they haven't been painted in some time and there is an area of damp above the small, barred window. Two very uncomfortable looking chairs take centre stage. Some B-list presenter that I recognise but don't know the name of strides from off camera, unbuttons his suit jacket and sits down. He reels off a monologue about how he has been granted unparalleled access to Johnny Mayhem. The self-importance is nauseating. He's mumbling to the camera about feeling nervous, hamming it up for the viewers by dabbing at his considerable forehead with a silk handkerchief, when a door at the far end of the room opens.

Johnny Mayhem emerges and is led to the vacant chair by a prison guard. Johnny thanks the guard, shakes the presenter's hand and nods a greeting at the assembled production team behind the scenes. This is the first time I have seen him since the final day of the court case, the one that found him guilty of murdering his wife. Gone are the rock star looks; his hair is now short and parted to the side, his unruly beard trimmed to stubble. The fog that had clouded his eyes seven years ago has also disappeared—his emerald eyes are piercing.

Johnny and the presenter, who introduced himself as Michael Sims, begin by discussing the night of the murder. Even after all these years, Johnny still professes his innocence; insisting that the police arrested the wrong person that night. When Michael asks if he had any idea who was behind his wife's murder, he shakes his head.

'I've thought about it every day for the past seven years and have always come up empty. It sounds like a cliché, but everyone adored Amanda. I can't think of a single person who would have wanted her…' Johnny struggles to finish the sentence. He opens and closes his mouth like a fish struggling for breath on land, before looking away from the camera. After a few moments, he looks back at the presenter and mumbles his apologies whilst wiping his nose with his sleeve. The program cuts to an advert.

'Jesus. He's going for the Oscar, isn't he?' Tom says, and I laugh. I agree with him. The clean-cut look, the pleasantries as recording began and the 'woe is me' attitude are on show for one reason and one reason only—to convince the watching audience to feel sorry for him. Any sympathy I'd felt creeping into my mind is quickly flushed away with the image of him sitting on the bed twirling the bloody baseball bat in his hands.

On the screen, the presenter has re-appeared and is talking again.

'How do you feel about the new witness coming forward?

'Extremely grateful,' Johnny replies. 'From what I've heard, it's far from conclusive, but my lawyer thinks we stand a good chance when we appeal.'

'And that's in a few days, right?'

Johnny nods his head.

'And how are you feeling about the possibility of being released from prison? About being proven innocent?'

A small smile creeps onto Johnny's face, though he quickly masks it. When he speaks, he looks at the camera with puppy dog eyes.

'Will it feel good that I've finally shaken off the 'wife-killer' tag? Absolutely. To know that you have been falsely accused is a horrible feeling. But, to know that your wife's killer is still out there somewhere, walking the streets as a free man, is torturous.'

'Do you have any ill-feeling towards the police?' Michael asks, the tone of his voice making it abundantly clear that he is hoping for a soundbite that he will be able to dine out on for years to come.

The camera switches back to Johnny and this time, the puppy dog eyes have disappeared, replaced with a look of fury.

'You know, the police were just doing their job, but they got it spectacularly wrong. I've tried for years now to let go of my anger. To forgive; to forget. But two names have orbited my brain since I was thrown in here.' He glances around the small room, as if to make his point, before looking back at the camera, glaring down the lens. 'Simon Black and Erika Piper.'

My heart skips a beat at the vitriol with which he spits my name. The presenter looks like he is close to climax and I can see him urging Johnny on. When Johnny doesn't speak, the presenter does.

'What have you got to say to Simon and Erika?'

Johnny snorts. His eyes still firmly fixed on the lens.

'They know they got it wrong and they should pay for that. The truth will come out. I'll make sure of it.'

He takes a deep breath and pushes himself out of the chair, motioning to the prison guard that he is ready to go back to his room. He doesn't even say goodbye to the presenter, though when the camera cuts to him, Michael looks delighted. A veiled threat to end the show is more than he could've hoped for in his wildest dreams. He is beaming as he bids the nation goodbye, urging us to tune in next time when the result of Johnny's appeal will be known.

'You okay?' asks Tom as he turns the television off.

I nod, though I'm not sure I am. The fact that Johnny has held my name in his head for so long is disconcerting. As I follow Tom up the stairs, Leo emits a shrill cry in the darkness that feels foreboding.

THREE MONTHS LATER

ROSES FOR THE DEAD

2

THE NEWS OF Johnny Mayhem's successful appeal had been in the headlines for twenty-four hours now and has continued to fill newspaper front pages and television screens today. News channels are replaying the footage of a smartly suited Johnny leaving court with a huge smile plastered on his face. The speech his lawyer had reeled off, pleading with the public to respect his client's privacy upon his release and demanding a full investigation into the murder of Amanda Mayhem, is also being played on loop. Pieces dedicated to trashing the police's work at the time have appeared in the less upmarket news outlets and a quick scroll through Twitter exposes huge swathes of vitriol towards anyone involved in the original case.

'Surely they can't let that murderer out of prison on the word of a junkie?' says Susie.

In the aftermath of the breaking news and personal trashing, it took all of my will power to leave the house to attend the meet up with my NCT group. Despite only knowing each other for the best part of ten months, stories of giving birth; stitches and leaking nipples are a quick way to cement firm friendships. After discussions about haemorrhoids, it feels like no topic is taboo. In the end, I'm pleased I did. It had taken my mind off the news, until now.

'There must have been enough evidence to clear his name,' I mumble. 'No judge is going to let someone walk free if there was even a hint of doubt.'

'But one newspaper said that the dealer only had a video that showed Johnny at his house earlier in the night. Sounds a bit sketchy to me,' she replies, pushing a strand of blonde hair behind her ear with one hand whilst shoving a spoonful of mushy vegetables into her son's open mouth.

'I bet he wouldn't have been released if he wasn't famous,' chimes in Lily.

'Do you think there will be some comeback on you?' asks Jill, rubbing sick off her shoulder and out of her hair with a wet wipe. The enormity of the question mixed with the levity of the act almost makes me laugh. Almost.

'I'm not sure,' I reply, shoulders slumping slightly. 'The DCI at the time; the guy in charge—Bob—has retired. I was the Detective Sergeant then, partnered with Simon Black, who was the rank above me, and he's left too. I imagine a new investigation will be opened into the death of Amanda Mayhem and the police will issue an apology to Johnny.'

'Will you be involved in the new case?'

I shake my head.

'No. When I go back after maternity leave, it'll be to the desk job I agreed to take after the murder-suicide case.'

My last case had been national news. The Guide, the presence behind the My Time to Die website, had helped people kill themselves as long as they agreed to kill someone else on their way out as repayment. I'd been the one to figure out who The Guide was and to bring him to justice.

Instinctively, I reach for my head and run my finger along the waxy scar—the one left behind when The Guide split my scalp open.

It had been my final case as a Detective Inspector, as Tom and I both felt that, with a baby on the way, it'd be safer if I retired from the action and focussed on the paperwork. A move that made sense, in theory, but one I still haven't come to terms with. It feels like all the hard work I had put in over the years—the selfish choices I'd made and the blinkered view I'd adapted to get to the top of my game was all for nothing. Wasted energy.

I blink the tears away before the other women can see them and look down at Leo, asleep in his pushchair. Leo, or Liam to give him his full name, is the only reminder I need when I'm feeling frustrated that, in fact, I have made the right decision. After getting stabbed in the stomach around five years ago, I'd been told that the chances of conceiving were implausibly low.

And yet, the little baby lying here beside me, chest rising and falling slowly, was proof that miracles can happen.

Last year, during my final case, the dangers of the job had been laid before me in stark black and white, and as Leo's eyes give a light flutter, I know I have made the right decision. Still, knowing you've made the right decision and coming to terms with it are two different things entirely.

We discuss the impending finish of our respective maternity leaves whilst hoovering up our lunches, before beginning the military grade operation of exiting the café with numerous pushchairs. We bid each other goodbye and I begin the short walk home, my thoughts on the job I'd loved and lost.

TOM SETS THE bowl filled to the brim with crisps on the table and throws himself onto the sofa beside me. He picks up the remote and selects the second episode of A Rose for the Dead. The program begins with a montage of news headlines from around the world—the same footage of Johnny Mayhem walking free from court that has been on loop for over twenty-four hours now.

I have mixed feelings about seeing him walk free. As part of the team that helped convict him in the first place, the feeling that he is innocent sits at odds with how convinced I was that he was guilty. I'd been at the scene of arrest. I'd seen Amanda's broken body and heard Johnny's howls of rage; the baseball bat turning malevolently in his hands. I'd studied the forensic reports; the information that only Johnny and Amanda's prints were present on the baseball bat imprinted on my brain. I'd seen Amanda's defensive injuries—deep purple bruises that had bloomed and spread across her forearms—and the broken bones in her hands. The house had shown no sign of forced entry and I knew that Johnny was the sole holder of a key, aside from his wife and a diminutive Latino cleaner they paid less than minimum wage for. The case was open and shut. It had to have been him.

And yet, new evidence had convinced a judge that it couldn't have been him. That he was elsewhere for part of the night. New evidence that had set a supposedly innocent man free. The gnawing feeling in my stomach that I'd experienced the whole way through episode one has returned. I'd put it down to nerves, about finding out how I'd be portrayed perhaps, but really, the feeling is guilt. I'd been part of the team that had consigned a man, wrongfully, to seven years in prison.

Michael Sims, presenter not-so-extraordinaire, sits on a plush, velvet chair, and stares into the camera. The top button of his shirt is unbuttoned, allowing dark hair to spill over the top. When he speaks, his tone is sombre.

'Ladies and gentlemen, welcome to the second episode of A Rose for the Dead.' He stops, and motions around at his surroundings. As the camera zooms out to reveal more of the room, it feels like a punch to the gut. 'We're here today, with Mr Johnny Mayhem; an innocent man, to discuss his feelings on release, redemption and reprisal.'

The chosen location for the interview is the bedroom in which Amanda lost her life. Aside from being cleaned of the blood which had splashed on the walls and drenched the carpet, the room remains the same. Johnny is sat on the bed, his arms behind him, holding him up.

The same bed he was sitting on all those years ago.

'Is this a fucking piss take?' I mutter to Tom.

'What do you mean?'

'He's sat in the same place he was after murdering his wife…'

'After finding her dead, you mean,' he interrupts. 'Remember, he was found innocent.'

I throw Tom a withering look.

'It's like he's trying to rub our nose in it. Trying to make a point.'

On screen, Michael has started his questioning.

'How does it feel to be a free man?'

Johnny looks around the room, at the expanse of luxury surrounding him, and breathes out a sigh.

'You know, it'd odd. For seven years, I had a routine and I had people around me. And now that I'm out, now that I've been proven innocent, being here feels more like a punishment. Being at home, without the love of my life, it feels wrong. My only wish now is that the police get their act together and get to finding the person responsible for Mandy's death.'

Michael nods his head sagely, revelling in the drama.

'And have you heard from anyone involved in the case that sent you to prison? Anything from the police?'

Johnny barks a hollow laugh. 'You must be joking. But, you know what? I don't really care. I've been proven innocent and that's all that matters. The world has finally seen me for who I am.'

'What do you have to say to your knight in shining armour? The man whose evidence has led to your freedom?'

On screen, a moment passes between the two men. Johnny looks annoyed at the question posed to him and the presenter wilts slightly under his stare. The show isn't live and I wonder why the footage was left in. When Johnny speaks, his face has reddened.

'Two things. I'd obviously like to say a massive thank you for coming forward but, of course, I'd question why it took seven years. The evidence was on that phone all along, and he let me rot in prison. Sorry,' he says, shaking his head and painting a smile back on. 'There are just a lot of different emotions to deal with right now.'

Michael hands him a tissue.

'Do you have plans to meet up with your saviour?

Johnny looks straight at the camera, venom in his eyes.

'Oh, I reckon our paths will cross again. In fact, I'm sure of it.'

3

I'M NOT CONCENTRATING on what I'm doing and wince at the sound of my alloys scraping against the kerb as I pull into the parking bay. Not a great start to a day I've already been dreading for months—the end of maternity leave. I look around at Leo in his car seat, smiling expectantly at me, and can feel a rush of contrasting emotions. I click the seat belt and get out, before I change my mind and simply drive home, pretending that work and life outside our little family bubble doesn't exist.

I get Leo out of his seat and pick up his cuddly lion toy, Sonya. Tom chose the name. He said since he couldn't be called Leo on account of the name already being used, Sonya was the obvious choice. And, ridiculously, it stuck. I grab the bag stuffed with back-up clothes, milk, dummies, and a multitude of other bits necessary to keep a small human alive and sling it over my shoulder.

Opening the gate whilst balancing so many items is a task in itself, and when I've made it into the small front garden and up the steps, I pause in front of the door. I exhale deeply and knock. There is movement inside; steps in a hallway and the metallic clinking of locks. The door swings open and I'm afforded a warm greeting, one that settles me slightly.

Clare, our godsend of a childminder, flashes a huge smile at me, before making a fuss of Leo and welcoming us in. We walk down the hallway and into a bright playroom. From the corridor, I can hear Clare locking the door and I'm pleased that she is so security conscious. She follows us into the room and sits on the floor, immediately picking out the toys Leo showed interest in when we were here for his settling in day. I set him on the floor and he treats Clare to a wide, gummy smile. She plays with him, pushing coloured blocks into a shape sorter, whilst going through their routine with me and checking his nap times and feeding patterns, pausing only to coo at Leo when he is demanding her full attention. Her meticulousness and her empathy remind me of how we felt upon meeting her for the first time, on the day when we'd visited many childminders and were less than impressed by most. Clare had stood out like a beacon in the fog.

She can see that I'm hesitating and assures me that Leo and her will have a lovely day, and that he'll be looking forward to seeing mummy at the end of her shift. She scoops him up and we walk to the door. I turn the key in the lock and blink back tears as I say goodbye to my little man. Clare pats my arm and tells me she will keep in contact; that she knows how hard the first day is. I nod my head, thank her and walk back towards my car.

I paint a smile on as I drive past her house and give a wave. Twenty metres up the road, I pull into another space and let it all out. The guilt I've been feeling about handing my baby over to a stranger surges out. I know everyone does it, and that he will probably have a brilliant time doing all sorts of activities and playing with toys he's never seen before, but it still feels unnatural. I console myself with that fact that Tom will be picking him up once his own shift is over, so he won't be there for the whole day, but still.

Pulling down the sun visor, I see that I've made a mess of my make-up. I set about making my face work-suitable and when I'm finished, head for the station.

'HOW ARE YOU DOING?' Sandra enquires, as I settle into my seat.

'Fine,' I say, looking around the basement office and trying to conceal my true feelings. Sandra is the office manager and has been known to take her role rather seriously.

'I know your heart is probably still on floor three,' she says, 'but the work we do down here is important too. I know the things they say about us up there.'

She rests a hand on my shoulder.

'You're one of us, now,' she adds, before walking away.

Creepy pep talk over, I survey my new desk and find a welcome back card and a lemon cupcake are awaiting me, along with a wrapped gift for Leo. The little surprise gives me a lift, and as I log onto the computer to check my job list, I think to myself that maybe this won't be so bad. That being out of the line of fire will be ok. As long as I can avoid Sandra.

By lunch, I've changed my mind. The most exciting thing on my agenda for today is making sure that information given to me in many manila folders is typed up and filed away. I've gone from a detective inspector, tasked with bringing murderers and rapists to justice, to being a glorified secretary, holed away on a subterranean floor.

A visit from DS Andy Robinson, the man I'd been partnered with in the aftermath of ghastly events during my last case, does nothing to cheer me up. In fact, it darkens my mood further. Hearing details of the case he's on is like Jim Bowen popping out of nowhere to show me what I could've won. He gauges my mood and mutters something about going for a drink soon to catch up, before scampering back to the lifts and returning to the promised land.

Once he's gone, I check my phone and flick through the photos that Clare has sent. One of Leo enjoying a mushed-up banana and another of him having a nap in a pushchair, his chubby legs dangling over the side. I set it down, my mood improved, and make a mental note to apologise to Andy for being blunt. Just then, the phone rings. After the briefest of conversation, I set the receiver down again and my improving mood heads south immediately. I lock my computer's screen, pick up my bag and walk towards the lifts with a heavy feeling in my stomach.

Being summoned by the DCI, whose team you are not technically on during your first day back at work, is not usually regarded as good. All sorts of things flash through my mind, though the most worrying one—the one with the flashing neon sign and the disorientating Wurlitzer music vying for pole position at the front of my brain—am I going to fired on the spot for my part in Johnny Mayhem's wrongful imprisonment?

I ascend in the lift to the third floor and when I walk out, I'm hit with a wave of nostalgia that momentarily stifles the worry. The stain on the carpet from where my former partner Liam once spilled two coffees simultaneously. The hubbub of busy people doing important tasks. My office, or rather, my former office, nestled in the corner of the room. Seeing it shouldn't bring back happy memories—God knows the hours that were spent in there poring over pictures of broken bodies and other macabre enterprises—but it does. It's not the grisly murders I miss, per se, but rather the sense of purpose that came along with it. The feeling that I was making a difference, getting justice for the victims.

Andy glances up from his computer screen and a look of confusion flashes across his face when we lock eyes. I point to the DCI's office and the confusion deepens. He holds his hands up and wishes me luck wordlessly as I make my way to Bob's old room. I knock and a brusque voice invites me in.

DCI Victoria Killick sits behind the same oak desk Bob and I had hashed ideas over for so many years. Instead of his considerable bulk, I'm greeted by a minuscule woman with pursed lips and a dark bob streaked with red. She nods a greeting and motions to a chair in front of the desk, which I duly sink into. She sets down the piece of paper she was perusing and fixes me with a look that I imagine has taken down many a hardened criminal, despite her size.

'Erika Piper, how lovely to meet you,' she says in a cockney accent, a small smile transforming her face from severe to friendly in an instant. She introduces herself and then takes a moment to look at me, sizing me up. 'How are things on the bottom floor?'

'Fine,' I lie, for the second time today. I don't want to appear ungrateful for a job I basically begged Bob to give me before he retired. Especially after only three hours of actually doing it.

I can see in her eyes, though, that she hasn't bought my mistruth.

'You are probably wondering why I've called you here,' she says.

I nod, unable to force my tongue into action.

'Well, I've been going over your file…' she starts.

And I don't hear much more. I know where this is headed. I zone out and think about all the free time I'll have. Perhaps, this is a good thing. The money I'll save on childcare would be a positive and I could also get round to finally painting the kitchen, too.

I'm brought back to the room when I catch the word exemplary.

'Sorry,' I interrupt. 'Exemplary? I thought you were firing me?'

She laughs.

'God, no. The opposite, actually. Erika, you are wasting your talents in the basement. Admin, though essential to the successful running of any organisation, is not for you. You have been instrumental in bringing some of the most horrible shits in the north west to justice.'

I realise then that I am staring at her, mouth open and jaw almost detached.

'Look,' she says. 'Yes, you were part of the team that got the Johnny Mayhem thing wrong. But, at the time, the jury bought it and the judge did too. You weren't the only one at fault. Don't carry that baggage around with you.'

She smiles kindly at me and I can feel the heat behind my eyes.

'To be forthright, because that's the type of person I am and forewarned is forearmed, there may be an enquiry into what went wrong with that particular case, but I can't see any of it landing on you. And, having read through all of the reports, I will fight your corner tooth and nail if anyone tries it on.'

My stomach drops at the thought of being investigated for any wrongdoing, but am pleased that Victoria has my back.

'Now, put that to the back of your mind and answer me this. Will you come back and be my DI?'

'I'M ASSUMING YOU said thanks, but no thanks?'

Tom sits opposite me at the dinner table, scooping spoonfuls of ice-cream into his mouth. I'd just about finished recounting my tale about the unexpected meeting with the new DCI when he'd shut me down.

'Well, actually, I told her I'd think about it.'

He sets his spoon into the empty bowl and looks up at me, fire blazing in his eyes.

'And what exactly is there to think about? You gave up the job in the first place because it's dangerous and you have a family now. Has something changed in the one day you were back in the building?'

'No, but...'

'Exactly. Nothing has changed. Criminals are still scum who will do anything if it means evading the police and Leo is still a little baby who needs his mother, alive.'

Now it's my turn to glare.

'You're being an arsehole,' I say, trying to keep my tone level. 'I know what the job entails. I know the risks, but I also know the rewards. I'm bored stiff in that office, after one day. How do you think I'm going to feel in a year's time?'

'Safe,' he replies.

I shake my head at him and exhale loudly through my nose, my frustration clear to see. I get up from the table, set my plate on the side and go upstairs. I go into Leo's room and watch him float through untroubled sleep, limbs splayed like a starfish. I lie down at the side of his cot and suppress a sob.

My predicament is so black and white to Tom. DI = danger. Office drone = safe. But that's not the way it works. His unwillingness to discuss it, to even acknowledge my unhappiness is very frustrating. I stay on the floor for a while until, resigned, I peel myself off the carpet and make my way to my own bed, pulling the covers over my head and blocking out the world.

4

'WHAT'S MORE IMPORTANT? The job or your family?'

Tom's last words as I'd shut the door after me play on repeat in my head. I'd walked out of the house mid-argument, frustrated at his refusal to see things from my side. It seems like all we've done since I broached the subject last night was fight about it. I fully get where he is coming from, but I've never been one to be dictated to. With my mind still swimming, I pull into the car park and walk towards my desk, hoping a few hours of mind numbing admin will help form a decision. Perhaps I'd not given the new, less exciting role a fair chance. I settle into my chair and start the computer to check the jobs list when the phone rings.

'My office, please, Erika,' comes the clipped voice of DCI Victoria Killick.

I set the phone down and get up, grabbing my bag, wondering if she'd been watching out her window for me and also if something had changed from yesterday. When I'd visited her in her office, she'd been sweetness and light, but from her tone today, it sounds like I've royally pissed her off somehow. Sighing, I walk to the lifts and press the button.

On getting out of the lift on the third floor, it's obvious something has happened. The room is a hive of activity. The frenetic click-clacking of computer keyboards and shouted instructions surround me as I shuffle towards the office I'd not visited in nearly a year, and have now been to twice in the same number of days.

When I knock on the door and enter, Victoria greets me with a little wave, whilst the other hand leafs through a folder on the desk. I sit down on the chair and wait for her to finish.

'How are you today?' she asks, closing the file and holding it to her chest.

'Fine,' I say. 'How are you?'

She ignores my question. 'Have you had enough time to think about what we discussed?'

I nod.

'I'd like to come back... but...'

'I could tell there was going to be a 'but' the moment you walked in,' she says, throwing the file onto the desk.

'I'm worried about how the job will fit with my family life. I really would hate to come back here and half-ass it because I can't juggle both sides how I need to.'

Victoria looks genuinely appreciative of my honesty.

'Okay, how about this,' she replies. 'You work the next case that comes in, and if at any stage you want out, or, if at the conclusion of the case you feel the role is no longer for you, you let me know and we can at least say that we tried.'

'Perfect.'

She stands, walks around the desk and offers her hand which I take in my own.

'Okay,' she says. 'Well, I'm pleased about that because we need you right away. Someone has just called in a body.'

I fight back a laugh.

'Are you serious?'

She gives me a look that tells me she is.

'I'm told that you were partnered with Andy before your maternity leave. I'd like you to work with him again. From what I've heard, you were a good team on the Clark case. He'll fill you in with what's happening.'

I thank her and walk towards the door. By the time my hand touches the handle, Victoria has picked up the telephone and is asking to speak to the head of the SOCO team. I smile at her efficiency.

I think I'm going to enjoy working under DCI Victoria Killick.

'HOW ARE YOU feeling about being back?' Andy asks, giving my shoulder a push.

I look out of my window at the passing cars, the trees and the vivid blue sky and reflect on my current predicament. I feel that by accepting my old job back, albeit on a semi-permanent basis, I'm cheating on my family and betraying Tom. Though, whizzing along the motorway towards a crime scene and a body, feels right. The little fizz of adrenaline is kicking in and the self-confidence required surges through me.

I know in my heart of hearts that I have made the right decision. This is what I was born for. Sadly, I'm not sure Tom will see it that way when I break the news to him later.

'I'm happy to be of use again,' I reply. 'What do we know about the body?'

Andy holds a finger up to show that he has heard me, indicates and pulls into the slip road to take us off the motorway.

'Not much. Just the address. Whoever phoned it in wouldn't give us a name, only the location. He also said there was a lot of blood, before hanging up.'

'No number?'

'Payphone, I think. Who uses a payphone these days?' he laughs.

'In this case, someone who doesn't want the police to know who they are. TV has shown everyone how easy it is to track a mobile.'

We spend the rest of the journey catching up about everything and nothing. I'd forgotten how easy it was to get on with him. It's jovial, but as we near our destination, a more professional atmosphere takes hold. I apologise for how I was yesterday, though he waves it away. A few minutes later, he indicates left and turns into a housing estate in the south of Ashton-under-Lyne.

The area reminds me of one of those trashy channel five programs with titles like *Britain's worst places to live* or *Shit tip Britain*. The council houses are small two-up, two-down, no nonsense affairs. Some have boarded up windows and show no sign of life. Long grass pokes over the top of rickety fences and on some of the doorsteps, men with grubby vests sit with a smoking cigarette between their lips and at least a week's worth of stubble on their cheeks. Some of the younger men on the estate polish pimped up cars parked outside their gates, the only thing in their life they are proud of. Grubby mattresses, broken children's toys and bags of rubbish litter most of the tiny front gardens.

Life here is not for dreamers.

Andy navigates through the rabbit warren and eventually we pull up at the crime scene, joining the fleet of other police vehicles. The house is the same as the others, though the garden is orderly and clean. The lawn has recently been cut and the bushes separating the garden from the neighbours trimmed, the green bin on the kerbside overflowing with grass and branches. Whoever lived here had not anticipated their sudden end.

A thin strip of blue and white plastic has been rolled across the width of the garden and a uniformed officer stands guard at the gate. A group of young lads ride by on bikes; some popping wheelies, most without helmets or their hands on the handlebars, all shouting some sort of abuse our way.

'Were you the first on the scene?' I ask the uniform, once the lads on bikes have left us to it.

'The area is known for trouble so there's always a car on hand,' he says, chewing his gum lazily. 'We were nearby and took the call.'

A number of the SOCO team are in the garden, and I follow their lead by pulling a forensic suit over my clothes and slipping foot protectors over my shoes. Andy and I sign the log book, recording what time we entered the crime scene, and walk up the path towards the open door.

The door leads straight into a poky living room. A cheap-looking fabric sofa, threadbare in places, rests against one wall. A bookshelf, filled mostly with biographies of sports stars, takes up a corner of the room and a huge television, resting on a wooden cabinet, blocks most of the light attempting to break through the window. A console whirrs noisily from one of the cabinet's shelves, its blue light flashing in the gloom. More of the forensic team are methodically searching the room, though Martin's less than dulcet tones float out from the kitchen.

We make our way through the doorway, pushing the beaded door curtain to one side. The kitchen is painted in a pale green and the cream cupboard doors look recently refurbished. A saucepan with sticky white rice residue and a single plate are in the sink, and an overflowing bin sits by the locked back door.

Martin is holding court. He's bent down, examining something on the floor. His bald head glistens with sweat, which often means he's on to something. He runs a gloved hand over his eyes, all the while barking orders at the small assembled team. When he hears the rustling of the beads, he looks up and locks eyes with me.

'I thought you were a desk grunt now?'

I smile at him. He's never had a filter.

'Change of plan,' I reply.

'Good, we need someone with balls and a proven track record on this one.'

That's as close to a *"nice to see you"* as it's possible to get from the man. Beside me, I can feel Andy bristle.

'What have you got in here?' I ask.

He ushers me closer and I follow his torch beam to the cupboards under the sink. It is filled with the usual cleaning products and rubber gloves, but there is also a small safe. One of the SOCO team has just finished picking the lock and the slightly bent door is lying open, revealing the treasure.

Inside is filled with multiple bags of different drugs. On first glance, I can pick out weed, coke, heroin and some small white pills, wrapped tight in clear plastic. A photographer takes a snap of the drugs in situ, before they are packaged and taken by one of the team to the van to be catalogued.

'Jesus,' I say. 'This guy was big time.'

'How much do you reckon it's worth?' Andy asks, directing his question to Martin, who puffs out his cheeks.

'Must be close to a million, I'd say.'

Well, at least now we have a motive for why someone might've killed whoever is waiting upstairs for us. If someone knew how much this guy's stash was worth, he was probably a pretty easy target. Drug dealers were notorious for trying to muscle in on each other's territory too, often resulting in gangland fights. There was probably no shortage of suspects.

'It doesn't look like anything was taken, though. The safe was piled to the top and it hadn't been opened before we arrived,' Martin adds, as if reading my mind.

'Unless he has another stash somewhere and they didn't know about this one,' I reply.

'Or,' Andy adds. 'whoever killed the dealer planned on coming back to take the drugs and then call in the body like a Good Samaritan?'

We let the theories come to rest as John Kirrane, forensic pathologist-extraordinaire pokes his head through the beaded doorway. His glasses have slipped down his nose and his ginger hair is as unruly as ever.

'Erika!' he says in surprise. 'I thought you were behind a...'

'Desk,' I finish his sentence for him, though not unkindly. 'I'm back. How long for? I don't know, but I'm definitely here for this one.'

'Great,' he says. 'A bit of experience always helps. Shall we go and see the body?'

I nod, following him out of the kitchen with Andy in tow.

'What do you think Martin meant about needing someone with balls?' Andy asks from behind me, and a smile creeps across my face.

5

I FOLLOW JOHN and the crime scene photographer up the carpeted stairs, past framed movie posters.

Sin City.

Death Proof.

Planet Terror.

That one has a woman wearing not very much with a machine gun in the place where one of her legs should be.

Ridiculous.

I think, gauging from these posters, I can guess the sex of the body we're about to uncover.

And then I laugh, which is wholly inappropriate, considering what I am here to do. But the posters remind me of Liam. He loved that type of violent, messed-up shit dressed up as arty noir.

The mixture of Andy declaring how much he loved Planet Terror and a thin slice of wood breaking off the banister and piercing my glove and thumb bring me back to the present. I swear at the sudden jolt of pain and John turns around from the step above to check what has happened. I hold up my torn glove and pull the splinter out by way of explanation, pocketing the sliver of wood so as not to contaminate the scene with my own blood. I pull the gloves off and replace them with a new pair as we reach the landing, which contains three doors, one of which is ajar and leads to a small bathroom. Another is wide open and shows a box room used as storage. Boxes overflowing with CDs and DVDs fill the floor and the bed is littered with clothes.

We open the door to the master bedroom and the scene of the crime. On the far wall, under a small window, rests an unmade single bed. A crime book, spine cracked and fanned out to save a page, lies on the pillow beside a partially torn condom wrapper. Drug paraphernalia is strewn across a small wooden desk—crack pipes, syringes and bent spoons. And in the middle of the floor is the body, slumped face-down in front of a two-seater sofa.

As I suspected, the body is that of a man. He is wearing a fitted black shirt and a pair of smart grey jeans—the word BOSS embossed onto a patch of leather on his rear. One of his trainers has slipped over his heel, exposing blue socks with cartoon hot dogs on them. His cropped blonde hair is sticky with blood and the fingers of his right hand are closed around a lavender rose. From under his body, the corner of a metallic tray pokes out.

An image of a lavender rose being clutched by Amanda Mayhem's pale hand glides into my mind.

'Well,' John says, 'I think cause of death is fairly obvious.'

He bends down next to the head and points to the small oval-shaped entry wound of a bullet. The photographer snaps pictures from various angles and distances, whilst John readies his tools. When the photographer gives him the thumbs up to show that he is finished, John inserts a rectal thermometer into the body. With this information, he will be able to work out how long the body has taken to reach the temperature of the room by using a simple equation and this will help with establishing a rough time of death.

When he is happy that he has got all he needs, John instructs us to turn the body. With as much care as we can manage, we roll him over so that he is flat on his back, next to the blood-soaked space where he was found.

Now that he has been moved, the metallic tray has been exposed. On it, mingled with blood, are the powdery remnants of cocaine. It is photographed and then removed from the scene.

The man's dead eyes face the ceiling and it's clear to see the hole near the bridge of his nose where the bullet left his body. One clean shot, almost professional in its precision, was enough to end this man's life.

I cast my gaze to the wall opposite and, as I suspected, there is a small hole just under a flat screen TV that has been fixed to the exposed brickwork. I point it out to the team. Martin will confirm it, but my suspicions tell me that the bullet will be buried in the brick.

My eyes trail over the rest of the body. His shirt had been unbuttoned down to his naval and a small razor blade is embedded just to the left of his tummy-button. The photographer takes more photos.

It's only when I turn my attention properly to his bloody face that I realise who it is.

His eyes, once so alive and now dulled by death, had gazed out of every newspaper a few months ago.

It was Duane Miller.

Johnny Mayhem's drug dealer.

The Duane Miller whose evidence got Johnny Mayhem released from prison.

The Duane Miller with whom Johnny Mayhem was sure his path would cross again.

And by the looks of it, their paths most certainly had crossed.

'What are we thinking?' Andy says, looking at me.

I tell the team who he is, though most have recognised him by now too. I take a moment to take in the scene again, before voicing my theory.

'Whoever did this…' I begin—it's important to keep an open mind at the beginning of a case, even though it may seem obvious who the perpetrator is. Saying "Johnny Mayhem did this," would only serve to focus our attention, perhaps incorrectly, in one area. Although, the lavender rose at the scene is no coincidence.

'I think we can assume that whoever did this was known to Duane. They were comfortable together,' I say, pointing to his open shirt. 'By the looks of it, Duane was sitting on the sofa, prepping a few lines of coke, when he was shot in the head from behind. I don't think he would have known what was happening. One shot was all it took; he fell onto the tray and the razor blade he was using to cut the coke got stuck in his stomach. Whoever did this, knew him.'

John nods his head in agreement. 'I think we can get the body out of here so that the SOCO team can comb the room.' He begins to make the necessary arrangements as I leave the room.

I SINK INTO the seat of the car and watch a SOCO team in the garden, methodically checking every nook and cranny for anything of worth. I pull the phone from my bag and find Tom's number before hitting the call button. It rings a few times before he answers, his tone light. It sounds like he's been laughing.

'How are you?' he asks.

'Fine,' I reply. 'How is everything at home today? How's Leo?'

'We're all good, aren't we little man?' he says, the pitch of his voice rising as Leo's giggles make their way down the phone. My heart skips a beat and a smile spreads over my face. 'We're just getting ready to head to the park. We thought we might swing by your way and we could have a family lunch. It's quite a nice day. I'll bring a picnic.'

'I'm not there.'

'What do you mean?' he asks. The lightness in his voice is gone.

'I mean I'm… They found a body. I was needed.'

A silence sits between us, thick as fog.

'You mean you took the job?'

'Yeah.'

'Fuck's sake,' he says, before disconnecting the call.

I try calling him again, but it goes straight to voicemail. I set the phone on my leg, just in case it was one of Leo's little wandering fingers that pressed the red button on Tom's phone, though I know that it's a rather naïve notion.

Tom wasn't to know the frenzied atmosphere in the office this morning, or the haste in which I made my decision, based on the shared adrenaline of the station's third floor. I'd explain to him later that it is on a one-case deal. Hopefully that will appease him.

Keen not to sink into a bad mood that may colour my work, I put the phone in my pocket, get out of the car and walk towards Andy, who is a few doors down, sitting on a low wall smoking a cigarette.

'Do you reckon it's him?' he asks, taking one last drag before throwing the butt on the floor and stamping on it.

'Mayhem?'

He nods.

'It's hard not to jump to that conclusion.'

I picture the last scene from the documentary, the scene where Johnny looked straight down the camera's lens and uttered those immortal words, charged with foreboding.

Oh, I reckon our paths will cross again. In fact, I'm sure of it.

'But,' I say, 'Duane was a drug dealer—a drug dealer with celebrity clientele. Why he lived in this shithole and not some penthouse in the city I have no idea. But, with him out of the picture, there are celebrities with too much money and too little sense who will be looking for a new dealer. We can't rule that angle out yet.'

'Leave all doors open, as my old DCI used to say,' he replies. 'Are we going to go knocking?'

I glance around at the houses; at the pulled blinds and closed minds, knowing full well the attitude the residents have towards police. Knowing that unless we catch someone on an off-day, no one is going tell us a single thing of note. But, that small chance is enough. It always is.

'I'll call a team in for that, but I would like to speak to the next-door neighbour personally. There's a chance he might've heard something.'

We push ourselves off the wall and walk up the path towards number 26. The curtains are closed and there looks to be no sign of life. I knock on the door anyway. After a few minutes, I knock again and a deep voice booms from somewhere inside.

'I'm coming for fuck's sake. Just give me a bloody minute to get there, ya bastard.'

A series of thumps tells me the occupant is storming down the stairs and when the door opens, it is almost pulled from its hinges. A bruiser of a man answers. At least six and a half feet tall. Shaved head. Tribal tattoos snaking around huge biceps and up the side of his neck, not quite reaching his face. Yet.

'What?' he barks. Andy and I both take an instinctive step back.

'My name is Detective Inspector Erika Piper and this is DS Andy Robinson. Can you start by telling us your name?'

'Mickey,' he replies.

'Let me guess,' Andy says, 'surname Mouse?'

'Johnson, actually. Smart arse,' grunts the giant.

'Mickey, we were wondering if you heard anything out of the ordinary last night?'

He shakes his head.

'It was business as usual. Loud music at all hours from that twat next door,' he says, jabbing a finger in the direction of the crime scene.

'Was he not a considerate man?'

'He's an arsehole. Parties all the time, people knocking on at all hours of the day, looking to score. I assume he's in some sort of trouble if you're here, disturbing me.'

'Duane Miller is dead.' I say.

'Right,' he replies, though he doesn't look like he cares too much.

'You're sure you didn't hear anything strange?'

He thinks for a minute. His hands massage his temples and he blinks sleepily.

'Well,' he says. 'Now that you mention it, at about three in the morning I thought I heard a gunshot. But, there's a load of knobheads around here with those big exhausts that backfire all the time and I put it down to one of those.'

'Three o'clock, you said?'

'About then,' he nods.

We thank him for his time and begin to step away from his house.

'One last thing,' I say, before he closes the door. 'Do you know who Johnny Mayhem is?'

He laughs.

'Of course.'

'Did you ever see him around here?'

'Are you kidding? He was in that house so often I thought he'd moved in.'

'Recently?'

'No, back before he was arrested. Him and Duane used to be best mates. Sad, really, your best mate being the man that sells you the shit that you poison your body with. Duane thought it would impress the rest of us, but it didn't, and we didn't have the heart to tell him that Johnny would move onto to someone else if it meant spending a bit less. I have never had much time for celebrities who think they are better than us mere mortals.'

I can't help but agree with Mickey.

'I've not seen him since he got out of jail, though. Small mercies. Now, can I do anything else for you, or can I go back to bed?'

We nod, he closes the door with force, and we walk back down the path towards the street.

'It still doesn't mean it's him,' I say to Andy, as we watch some of the SOCO team drive away.

'But it's sounding more and more like it is,' he replies, and I nod, the lavender rose unignorable.

6

ANDY AND I leave the lift on the third floor and walk through the office. I peer into my old office to find it unoccupied, though there is a bunch of flowers sitting on the desk. The name plate hasn't been changed either.

'Do you reckon it's still mine?' I ask.

'I think so. They've not managed to recruit permanently, so I assume it's still your space. I tried to put dibs on it but Vicky shot me down.'

He wanders off to his own desk while I open the door and walk in, lifting the bouquet of carnations to my nose and allowing the scent to take over my senses. I set them back down and check the label, assuming Tom had them sent over by way of an apology. I'm surprised to find they are from DCI Killick, or simply Victoria, as she has signed it, with a short welcome back message. I'm incredibly touched. For her to have the thoughtfulness to do that during a murder enquiry, it really makes me feel part of the team again.

Valued, again.

I set the flowers on the side and am just about to find a vase for them when my phone rings.

'Martin, hello,' I answer.

'Hi, Erika. Are you back at the station?'

When I confirm that I am, he tells me not to go anywhere—that he's got something I'll want to see and that he'll be with me shortly. When he hangs up, I walk to the kitchen and look for a vase, eventually finding one under the sink behind some ancient cleaning products with the seals still very much intact.

I walk back to my room, arrange the flowers in the vase, pour in the flower food that came with the bouquet and set it on the side. My computer is just powering up as Martin knocks on my office door and lets himself in. Andy follows him in holding two cups of tea.

'Martin, sorry, I didn't know you were coming in. You want me to go and make you one?' he says, handing me one of the mugs.

'Nah, you're alright, son,' he says. 'We've got more pressing matters here.'

He sits down in one of the chairs in front of my desk, plonking his bag on the floor. He unzips it and pulls out three clear evidence bags. The first has a small bullet in it. The tip has been blunted by the impact with skull and wall, but the shine remains on the bottom half.

'This is the bullet that was in the wall,' Martin says. 'Single bullet. One shot. Dead. It's a 9mm. I reckon, taking into consideration the depth with which it was embedded in the brickwork, we're looking at a mid-range handgun. Nothing fancy.'

'And there was no sign of the gun in the house?'

He shakes his head.

'No. Some of the lads are still over there so it might turn up. But I think whoever killed him either brought it themselves and took it back with them, or else used Duane's own gun on him and got rid of it. Be good to talk to some of his mates to find out if he was carrying. Drug dealer on that scale is gonna have a gun, isn't he?'

'You'd assume so,' I nod. 'Get your lads to look in the bins in the estate. Whoever did this…'

'Mister Mayhem,' Martin interrupts.

'We don't know that,' I say, though I don't sound convincing. 'Whoever did this might've chucked the gun at the first chance they got. Get in touch with the council and tell them to hold off emptying the bins until we tell them to.'

He takes out his notebook and writes the words council and bins. If it were anyone but Martin, the brevity of the notes wouldn't fill me with confidence. As it is, he tucks the pen behind his ear, and I know it will be done.

'I'll get the bullet fingerprinted, just in case. If this *was* a spur of the moment thing, someone might've got careless.'

He puts the bullet carefully into his bag and turns to the second piece of evidence.

'His phone,' he says, holding the bag up, revealing the latest model iPhone. When held vertically, a light comes on, showing the need for a four-digit passcode to gain access.

'Is it Duane's?'

'I think so. It's his picture on the home screen. Though, obviously we can't get into it without the code.'

'Get it to Ross Powell. He'll have it unlocked in no time.'

'No problem,' he says, putting it in the bag alongside the bullet.

'What's the last thing?' I ask, pointing at the final evidence bag sitting on my table.

'This is the puzzling one. It was found in the victim's pocket.'

He hands me the bag. Inside is a brushed silver pocket watch with a white face, the hands stopped at seven o'clock. A red capital S held inside a small black square sits underneath the 12 on the clock's face. Presumably the logo of the manufacturer. A thin chain snakes its way to the bottom of the bag. There are words on the back, elegantly engraved.

Time will take us all.

'Strange,' I say, snapping a picture of the face and the inscription, before handing the watch back to him.

Why would he have it in his pocket if the batteries had stopped working? Was it an affectation? Or had they stopped that day and he hadn't noticed before putting it inside his pocket?

'Good work, Martin. Hopefully this will all lead to something.'

He gets up and leaves the room with a small nod.

'Now what?' Andy asks.

'Now, we wait for Ross to work his magic with the phone and hope that it gives us something.'

My phone rings and Andy excuses himself before I answer. When I do, Victoria starts talking straight away.

'Erika, I heard about the victim. If we're to assume that Johnny Mayhem could be behind this, we need to consider that he may have other targets. You, being one of them. We need to take precautions. When on the job, make sure you always have a partner. No lone-wolf stuff. I'm also arranging an unmarked car and plain clothes officers to watch your house overnight.'

'There's no need...' I begin.

'There's every need,' she interrupts. 'You're no good to us dead. It's happening, no arguments.'

She cuts the call. No arguments.

'LOOK,' TOM SAYS, setting down his fork so that he can pick up the bowl Leo has just knocked off his high chair's tray onto the floor. 'I'm not angry.'

'You sounded it earlier.'

He mops up the mush with a wet wipe and pushes it into the bin, before sitting back down and taking my hands in his.

'I'm really not. I'm just worried. We're a family now. You've got what you always wanted, what you thought you could never have.'

We both turn our attention to Leo, who is rubbing the spoon with orange pulp in it onto his scalp whilst beaming at us, showing off a gummy smile.

'I know. And I thought that once we had him, I'd feel different about the job. I thought I'd be scared on the streets and that I'd feel safe behind a desk. But, I'm not. If anything, I'm even more aware of the evil in the world and I know that I can make a difference.'

He smiles at me.

'And it's on a one job basis?'

I nod. 'Just to see how I feel.'

'And what if you like how it feels?'

I shrug and he gets up, taking our empty bowls into the kitchen and returning with a glass of water.

'What about us? About him?' he says, pointing to Leo. 'Don't we get a say in this?'

'Of course you do,' I counter, my voice rising. 'He's the most important thing in my life, but I can't just give up being me and waste my life in a job I hate.'

'Like I did,' Tom replies quietly.

'That's not what I meant.'

Our argument is interrupted by the unmistakable squelchy sound of Leo filling his nappy.

'I'll take him up. It's bedtime anyway.'

Tom stands up and frees Leo from his high chair. I stand too and envelop my boys in a group hug. I can feel Tom's hand squeezing my shoulder and Leo's mucky fingers comb through my hair. They go upstairs and I flop back in my chair, realising that the situation could quickly become like Groundhog Day; neither of us willing to budge, neither willing to back down.

It's only for one case, I tell myself.

Though, already, I know that it probably won't be.

A sigh escapes my lips and I stand to clear up the mess that Leo has left behind. I tip the remnants of the meal into the bin and load the plates and cutlery into the dishwasher, before starting it with a beep. I pour myself a glass of wine and walk into the living room, clearing away the toys on the floor whilst listening to the news. Victoria has scheduled a press conference tomorrow about Duane's death and so far, thankfully, word hasn't got out. If we can keep the press at bay, it will help the investigation tenfold.

Once the room is habitable, I sit on the sofa and find the second episode of the A Rose For The Dead documentary. I watch the smarmy presenter introduce the show and then fast forward to the section where Johnny is questioned about the drug dealer's evidence that freed him. Once more, I watch as his face reddens, his anger apparent. And then he opens his mouth.

'Two things. I'd obviously like to say a massive thank you for coming forward, but I'd question why it took seven years.'

Seven years.

Seven.

And I make a connection.

The pocket watch with the unmoving hands—stopped at seven o'clock. And that strange inscription.

Is it a clue or simply a coincidence?

I get out my phone to call the station, to tell Victoria about my theory when I see that I have a missed call from Ross Powell. I hadn't realised my phone was on silent. I check my voicemail but he hasn't left one. He never does. I return the call and press the phone to my ear.

'Hello,' he answers.

'Sorry I missed your call, Ross, everything okay?'

A crunching noise sounds down the phone that sounds like static. I check the screen but it shows that we are still connected.

'I think I'm losing you,' I say.

'No, you're fine, I'm just eating crisps.'

'Jesus, you're always eating when we talk.'

'I'm always eating, full stop,' he laughs. 'Don't think I'm going to stop just 'cos I'm talking to a pretty lady.'

'What do you have for me?'

'Well,' he says, pausing to suck crisp dust from his fingers by the sounds of it, 'I managed to unlock the phone.'

'Well done—that was quick. Did you have to use some of your fancy equipment?'

'0420,' he says.

'0420?' I repeat.

'That was the code. I tried 1234 and 0000. 0420 was my third try and it worked.'

'Why 0420?'

'It's some drug thing—some sort of number to do with appreciating marijuana. You'd think he'd try harder though, wouldn't you?'

'Thankfully for us, he seems like a bit of a numbskull,' I say. 'Anything useful?'

'I've downloaded all the messages onto the server for you. Most of them are just "customers" arranging deliveries, but there's one that I think you're going to be very interested in.'

I can feel my stomach bubble.

'Oh yeah?'

'Yeah,' he says. 'There's a message from Johnny Mayhem inviting him to Havana.'

'Cuba?'

'No, dickhead,' he laughs. 'That celeb nightclub in the city centre. Duane agreed to go and they arranged to meet there at ten o'clock last night.'

My pulse quickens.

'And then he was dead a few hours later. Thanks, Ross.'

'Anytime,' he says, before hanging up.

I immediately call Victoria, who listens carefully as I tell her about the watch/documentary connection and the information I've just learned from Ross. She assures me that any follow up action can wait until everyone has been briefed in the morning. She ends the call by telling me she's pleased I decided to come back and to get a good night's sleep. That I'm going to need it.

7

WE PULL INTO the car park of Manchester Royal Infirmary and find a space easily enough, a rare occasion in a hospital car park. I get out and walk over to the ticket machine, shoving a multitude of coins in to pay the extortionate price for our relatively short stay. I take the printed ticket and place it in the windscreen of the car, to keep the parking attendants at bay. I'd heard of police officers leaving a note in the car explaining why they were there in lieu of payment, but it felt like a dick move considering hospital staff were still expected to pay for the luxury of parking on site to do their jobs.

We enter the hospital, walk past a bored looking receptionist who is leafing through a glossy gossip magazine and make our way down the pale blue corridors towards the mortuary. I press the button beside the doors, accessible only by authorised personnel pressing a key card to the black box mounted on the wall, and hear a buzzer sound in the space behind. Seconds later, the door is opened from the inside by someone I've never met before.

'We've been expecting you Miss Piper,' he says with a wide smile, 'and you, Mr Robinson.'

Andy and I exchange a puzzled glance and follow the man inside, towards John Kirrane, who is in his office. The young man steps back and lets us enter first, before following us in. John looks up from his computer screen and looks sternly at the man.

'Mr Maston, have you offered Miss Piper and Mr Robinson a drink?' he asks, his tone terse.

The man stammers.

'I'll assume that is a no. I thought we'd been over this when our first set of visitors arrived this morning. I'm not in the habit of repeating myself, though I will make a special exception for you. Go and make three teas, now.'

A sweating Mr Maston leaves in fast forward and is barely out the door when John breaks into fits of childish giggles. For a man nearing sixty, it's a disconcerting sight.

'It's his first day,' he explains. 'Harry Maston. Fresh out of university; green around the gills, and I'm giving him a bit of a hazing. I've told him we must address each other formally and that he must write down any questions he has, rather than ask them verbally.'

'You're a cruel man,' I say, over the roar of Andy's laughter.

'I've not got it in me,' John laughs. 'I've nearly caved a couple of times. Harry's a nice lad—eager to please and he seems to know what he's doing.'

'What happened to Trevor?'

'My old assistant got offered a job at St. Thomas down in London. He's from that way so it made sense to be close to family.' He finishes tapping on his computer, locks the screen and stands up. 'Are we ready?'

I nod and walk out of the office into the open space of the mortuary, just as Harry bundles through the door with three teas in a cardboard holder. He hands a cup to me, Andy and John.

'Did you not get yourself one?' I ask.

'Mr Kirrane said to get three,' he says, shrugging his shoulders.

I turn around to look at John and can see from the expression on his face that he feels bad. I turn back to Harry.

'You've got to toughen up, mate. He's fucking with you.'

Harry looks over at John, who nods and breaks into wild fits of laughter. At first, Harry looks lost but soon joins in with the merriment.

'You bastard,' he sniggers. 'I thought I'd made the biggest mistake in the world in accepting this job!'

John steps forward and shakes his hand, apologising for taking the piss, though Harry waves it away. It seems John has found his new partner in crime.

Once the laughter has died and the mortuary gowns and foot covers have been pulled into place, the jovial atmosphere disappears and the respect the dead deserve settles back over the room. The constant hum of the body storage cabinets, alongside the whirr of the air conditioning, are noticeable now; a physical coldness mirroring the job we're about to undertake.

In the middle of the room, lying on a metal table under bright lights, is the body of Duane. His brother, Jared, had attended the hospital this morning to formally identify the body. As a well-heeled banker who had managed to turn his unhappy upbringing around, Jared had apparently been unsurprised at the violent end his brother had met. He had simply given the body a cursory glance, confirmed it was Duane and left without so much as a backward glance or show of emotion.

'Harry,' John says. 'If at any stage you need to leave the room, I understand. There's no shame and there will be no judgement.' He smiles warmly at his new technician, who reciprocates, though he does already look a little grey.

John moves over to the console at the side and starts the recording. The modern mortuary has microphones built into the ceiling tiles. Over the years, I'd watched John speak any detail he thought pertinent as he circled the body, anything he thought might help avenge the dead. Many of those details had.

Today, he starts by stating who is present in the room, the name of the victim and the date and time of the post-mortem.

John then tells Harry which parts of the body need photographing. As this is first real body Harry has dealt with, this part of the process takes longer than usual, though John is very patient and directs him with kind words and a calm tone. When finished, he pats Harry once on the shoulder and the young man's chest puffs out slightly. So far, so good.

While Duane's body is swabbed and removed of its clothes, I stare at his face; at his open eyes and at the exit wound of the bullet that ended his life. I think about the path that led him here. He must've considered himself set for life once he got into dealing for celebrities, leaving the shitmunchers and the junkies behind. He must've been rubbing his hands when it was his evidence that freed Johnny Mayhem from prison—at the thought of the kudos that was about to head his way. And yet, a couple of weeks later, here he is.

I watch as John circles him, noting everything he can see. At various times, he calls for Harry to provide him with an evidence bag. The latest is for scrapings from under Duane's fingernails. Flecks of white are tipped into a plastic tube, the top sealed and placed into a bag. Harry places a sticker with Duane's details on the front of the bag before stepping back and watching, trying to anticipate John's next need.

'He died where he lay,' John says. 'There was no movement post mortem.'

John motioned to the body, the livor mortis obvious even to the casual observer. The front half purple, the back white. It was to be expected, having been at the crime scene, but it was useful to have the evidence to say so. The blood in the body that hadn't escaped through the bullet's exit wound had settled in the front half of the body, the side that had been in contact with the floor.

Aside from where the razor blade had cut into the abdomen, which John measures and Harry photographs, there is nothing else suspicious on the front of the body. When happy that every scrape and bruise has been accounted for, the body is turned over.

The white side of the body is in good shape, aside from the hole in the back of the head. Duane was obviously a fan of the gym, his wide back muscular and lean. We gather around the head at John's request and take it in. Dried, dark blood surrounds the bullet hole, making it seem wider than it actually is. John carefully measures the entrance wound, just to make sure that the bullet embedded in the wall was the same one that passed through the head and not from another dispute some time ago. Harry takes a few photographs before John speaks.

'The bullet entered the parietal bone and exited through the frontal bone. Slight deviation in its course, which is natural, of course, given what it had to travel through.'

Once he is happy, the body is then ready for its internal examination. I watch Harry's chest rise and fall a little faster as

John walks towards the tools of his trade. The body is turned again, and John begins by making a cut on the torso.

The post-mortem passes in timely fashion. Harry nips out as the bone saw is fired up, but to his credit, returns as a section of skull is removed, giving access to the brain. John gives him a thumbs up just before he delves into the grey matter.

'Well,' he says, as we walk into his office, post-mortem complete, 'aside from the bullet to the head he was in very good shape. Nothing internal to warrant any suspicion.'

'So, the cause of death was the bullet?' I ask, already sure of the answer.

'Yes, causing massive trauma to the brain,' John confirms. 'The blood work will take a few days, and I don't usually like to colour in with shades that I don't have, but I would suspect that there will be traces of drugs and alcohol in the system.'

I nod my head in agreement.

'I'll get the full report over to you as soon as it is ready. Do you think it's Mayhem's work?'

'Early signs would suggest he's in the running.'

'Say no more,' he interrupts. He knows how I don't like to assume anything with so little to go on. 'So, what's next?'

'We're going clubbing,' I say. When I'm met with a blank face, I explain about Mayhem's text message invitation to Duane.

'Good luck!'

We thank him, de-robe and head towards the door. Just outside, a very white Harry is sitting bolt upright on one of the waiting area's chairs. He looks our way out of the corner of his eyes as we exit the mortuary and gives us a weak smile.

'You did good, kid,' says Andy, patting his shoulder on the way past. I stop and bend down so that I am eye level with him.

'For your first, you were amazing. I've seen veteran police officers duck out and not come back. You've got balls, Harry. You're going to be just fine.'

I push myself up using the arm of the chair and walk towards Andy, who is nearing the exit.

'Oh, and Harry?' He turns to look at me. 'Don't take any more shit from the old man.'

He laughs as I follow Andy outside.

8

HAVANA, MANCHESTER'S NEWEST, trendiest nightclub for the rich and famous, is in the Northern Quarter area of the city. Simple, metallic letters spell out the club's name above a set of tall, wooden doors. Elaborate stained glass windows are built into ornately carved stone walls; a reminder of the buildings more holy, original purpose. Havana is currently the place to be seen if you were anybody, much like how All Star Lanes had enjoyed a period of time in the spotlight after Rihanna and Drake had paid a late-night post gig visit. Celebrities had been stumbling out of this club for the past few months, but who knew how long it would be before they found another haunt and this place was done for.

We walk up the steps and hammer on the door. An officer from the station had phoned ahead and arranged a meeting with the manager, so we knew someone was inside. A series of scrapes sound from behind the door and then it swings open. The man in the doorway brings his hands up to his face, in an attempt to keep the sun out of his eyes.

'Are you the police?' he asks.

We confirm that we are and he ushers us inside.

Clubs always confuse me in the daytime. The lack of bodies, music and pulsing lights render it a sad sight. The wooden beams, possibly the original flooring from the church or a very good reconditioned job, look out of place. Everything else is either black or white, and modern. A large dancefloor area fills the middle of the room, high tech lighting connected to rigging on the ceiling. Sleek, black leather sofas fill one wall and a well-stocked bar runs the length of the other. A wide-ranging selection of optics hang from the wall and colourful drinks fill the fridges. A large wine rack is displayed behind the translucent bar. Semi-circular booths at the rear of the room are separated from the dancefloor by red, velvet ropes. It's tastefully decorated and I can see why it has become the flavour du jour.

The same cannot be said for the man in front of me.

Long, straggly hair falls over one of the palest faces I've ever seen. Dark stubble grows in patches along his jawline and his knitted jumper and tracksuit bottoms combo could not be more out of place within the lavish walls of the nightclub. He motions to one of the booths at the back and we follow him. He unhooks a rope from its holder and ushers us onto the plush sofa, which I sink into. He leaves the rope to flop onto the floor and joins us, sitting opposite.

'So, you're the manager?' Andy asks, taking out his notebook and setting it on the table.

'Indeed, I am,' he replies. 'Tony Marshall.'

'Well, thank you for your time,' I say. 'We're hoping you can help us with something.'

I notice that he looks a bit worried as I reach into my bag and pull a picture of Duane out. The picture was lifted from one of his social media pages and shows Duane in a Hawaiian shirt with his arm around another man. I push it across the table towards Tony who picks it up and smiles.

'It's my man, D.' He glances up at us and seemingly remembers who he is talking to. 'Ah, Duane Miller.'

'And who is he exactly?'

He falters for a few seconds. 'Duane is uh… a philanthropist…'

'We know he was a drug dealer,' Andy interrupts. 'Was he a friend of yours?'

'Let me make it very clear to you, I don't do drugs. Duane comes here because he is a ray of sunshine. People love him. The clientele of this place love him. We made it very clear to him that no deals were to be done in the club—and he never has.'

'Mr Marshall, I'm sorry to have to be the one to tell you, but Duane Miller was killed last night.'

He rubs the back of his head before covering his mouth with his hand. 'Fuck,' he mutters, sinking back onto the comfortable sofa.

'We're hoping you can help us,' Andy says.

Tony nods his head and sits back up.

'Where were you last night at three o'clock?' I ask.

'You don't think I've got anything to do with this?' he replies, his eyes wide. When I don't answer, he does. 'I was here until five this morning. Clearing up after the revelry. That's why I look like shit. I'm pale as a fucking vampire because I come here at night and sleep in the day.'

'And I'm imagining someone can vouch for you?'

'Yeah,' he nods. 'There were others here with me. Kacy locked up with me and I'll be on CCTV. We have interior cameras which we leave rolling.'

'Was Duane here last night?' Andy asks.

Tony nods.

'Was he here with Johnny Mayhem?'

This time, Tony shakes his head. 'I ain't seen Johnny in a few days now. The first couple of weeks after getting out of jail, he was here most nights. He was here so often that the journos out front stopped taking pictures of him. The papers were chock full of him, stumbling out of the club with a different girl on his arm, but after a month of it, no one was interested anymore. When he stopped coming, I was shitting my pants that some other club in the city had become the celebrity hotspot and he'd abandoned us. But it seems he's gone to ground. No one has seen him since.'

'So, who was Duane here with?'

'Well, he found me and asked if Johnny was here, but I told him that he wasn't. The guitarist from The Darling Roses was here though. They got a booth, this one actually,' he says, 'and spent the rest of the night drinking.'

'Does the guitarist have a stupid name like Mayhem too?' Andy says with a laugh. 'Let me guess… Lorenzo Diamond? Clive Rectangle? Chet Machete?'

'Lazarus Lazer,' replies Tony.

My face falls.

'Nah, I'm fucking with you,' Tony says. 'His name is Glenn Lumb.'

'Glenn Lumb?' I repeat, writing it into my notepad so that we can follow up with him. 'Jesus, he'd be better off with Lazarus Lazer.'

'Have Johnny and Duane been here together since he got out of jail?'

'Yes.'

'And...' says Andy, circling his hand in the air, inviting Tony to continue.

'It was last weekend. Maybe the last time Johnny was here actually. Johnny walked in, drunk as a skunk, and walked straight up to Duane. Things became... fractious.'

'Fractious how?'

'They started to argue. Which isn't good for business, so I went over and separated them. I was going to chuck Johnny out but he left of his own accord.'

'Was that typical of Johnny?'

'Since he got released? Yeah. He was a heavy drinker before jail and he's picked up where he left off.'

So, Johnny and Duane had had an altercation the last time they had seen each other. Was Johnny's text message an attempt at reconciliation or was it to lure the drug dealer here as part of his death? Did Glenn Lumb have something to do with it? Were Johnny and him in cahoots with each other?

'Look, Duane was a good dude. Yes, he sold drugs, but he was alright. He didn't deserve to die,' Tony says, sombre. 'Is there anything else I can help you with?'

'Two things actually,' I say. 'One, I need the CCTV from last night...'

'No problem, I can e-mail that across now.'

'Thank you. And two, do you know how I can get in touch with Glenn Lumb?'

'I do actually. I don't have his number or address or anything, but he's doing a signing in HMV tomorrow, in the Arndale Centre. You can head down and see him there.'

We thank him for his time and walk towards the door.

'You know,' he says as he opens it for us. 'You should come down sometime. I'll make sure you don't have to queue…'

We thank him again and leave.

'What do you reckon, boss?' Andy asks as we get into the car.

'I only wear pyjamas past eight o'clock now, so I don't think I'm their clientele.'

He laughs as the phone rings.

'Hello?' I answer.

'Erika, we have the murder weapon.'

THE BRIEFING ROOM is full to capacity. All the seats have been taken and standing space is at a premium. As ever, it is boiling. I curse the architect's short-sightedness at not having air con installed as I slip my jacket off and slide it under my chair.

Victoria takes to the front of the room and silence descends.

'Since the press conference this morning, the media have been hounding me for more information. It seems mentioning Johnny Mayhem was a mistake…'

'Or, a stroke of genius,' says a uniformed officer. 'If the media are hunting for him too, he's bound to turn up soon.'

'Thank you for that,' she says with a warm smile. 'I hope you're right. Unfortunately, it also means they'll be crawling all over this story like flies on shit. Everything we do will from here on out will be scrutinised and time is now of the essence. Erika is going to lead this and get everyone up to speed.'

She hands the floor to me. I stand up and walk to the case board, pointing to the picture of the victim.

'The victim's name is Duane Miller,' I announce to the room. 'Drug dealer to the stars. He may look familiar to you as it was his evidence that freed Johnny Mayhem from prison. At least, I *hope* that's why he looks familiar.'

This elicits laughter from the crowd.

'A bullet to the back of the head killed him. We think whoever shot him…'

'You mean Mayhem?' says someone in the back row.

'We'll get to that in a minute,' I reply. '*Whoever* killed Duane was probably known to him. He was shot once from behind, close up, in his own bedroom, so this wasn't a sneak attack. Martin is going to talk to you about the gun used shortly.'

I can see the head of the SOCO team shuffle uncomfortably from foot to foot at the side of the room. Despite having a big mouth on him at a crime scene or in the pub, he's notoriously shy and doesn't enjoy talking to a room full of police officers.

'Regarding Johnny Mayhem,' I continue. 'We know that he and Duane had a public argument last week in Havana, and we also know that Johnny made a vaguely threatening comment in that documentary. It was him who invited Duane to the club last night. We found a text message on Duane's phone, however according to the manager of the club, Johnny never showed. One of his ex-bandmates did, however, so we are going to follow that up.'

Victoria takes a few steps towards the centre of the room.

'We're not putting all our eggs in one basket with this. We know that Amanda Mayhem was holding a rose when her body was found and Duane was also found holding one last night. It's looking likely that Johnny is involved somehow, but we're keeping an open mind. With that in mind, we've set up a telephone hotline, in the hope that any sightings of Mayhem will come straight through to us, so that we can act on them immediately. I've already earmarked officers to be part of that team. I know we'll probably get a load of crank calls, but I've seen it work before. Johnny is a celebrity, so he can't go around without being noticed.'

She takes a few steps back as I welcome Martin to the front of the room. He nods at me as he passes, before pressing a button on the remote, causing the flat screen monitor attached to the wall to spring to life. On it, is a picture of a gun, inside an evidence bag.

'We found this in a bin on the estate,' he says. 'It's a Walther PPQ M2—a semi-automatic pistol that's seemingly favoured by the gangs of Manchester at the minute. It's small enough to be easy to conceal, but it's also powerful enough to kill from a distance. The clip had three more rounds in it and the bullets are a match for the one we found in the wall at Duane's house— the bullet that killed him. His fingerprints are on it, alongside a host of others, presumably his friend's. Working theory is that it is his own gun and that someone saw an opportunity. Mayhem's prints are not on it, but if he knew he was going to the house to kill, he would've been prepared. He would've worn gloves.'

He addresses the team of uniforms who were handed the short straw—knocking on doors in the estate where Duane lived in the hope that someone had seen something and was feeling loose lipped. 'Anything?'

'A lot of getting told to fuck off,' says one man, whilst the others shake their heads.

'As expected,' Martin says. 'Still, it was worth a go. A forensic team are still at the scene so if anything pops out to me, I'll fire an email round.'

The meeting winds down with one clear message.

Johnny Mayhem *must* be found.

9

THE QUEUE OUTSIDE HMV can't be what Glenn Lumb had been hoping for. Branded plastic tape, similar to police tape, has been used to section off a lane of the top floor, so that other shoppers don't become intermingled with the crowd. Whichever poor HMV employee had been handed that task needn't have bothered.

About thirty people in total, myself and Andy included, have turned out for the signing session. We're the last to join the line, which barely makes it out the door. A few shoppers poke their head in to see who it is, before noticing a poster with Glenn's face on it and walking away, mumbling about how they have never heard of him or that they thought he'd retired a long time ago.

A life in the spotlight is fleeting, however hard you try and hold on to it. An ageing rocker trying to flog CDs is no match for the power of Spotify or TikTok, or whatever it is the kids are using these days. Truthfully, Glenn's music is not for me either. If it weren't for the case, I wouldn't be aware of his existence. Tom had played a few of his song's last night when I told him that I was meeting him today, but it wasn't to my taste. I'm more of an ABBA girl. Though, having watched Teresa May's Alan Partridge-esque dance moves a couple of years ago as she sashayed painfully across a stage to 'Dancing Queen' changed things in my head somewhat. Through no fault of their own, my love for the Swedish foursome has been slightly tainted.

Another few people join the queue behind us just as Glenn Lumb emerges from a door near the tills to a ripple of applause. He walks to the signing desk with the swagger of a Gallagher and takes his place, pen in hand. I watch him as he greets his fans with a genuine smile. He spends a minute or two with each, signing whatever they've brought, posing for photographs and chatting happily before repeating the process with the next in line.

When it is our turn, we sidle up and greet him. He flashes a smile but looks confused at our empty hands.

'Forgotten to buy the album or what, lass?' he drawls in his thick Mancunian accent.

'No,' I say. 'We're actually from the police. I'm DI Erika Piper and this is DS Andy Robinson. Is there any chance we could have a word?'

'Are you joking, love?' he laughs. 'I'm a bit tied up here.'

'We could always do this at the station.'

'I've had enough of police stations in my time, thank you very much. Let me finish up here and then we'll go for a coffee.'

We move away and let the real fans have their turn with the guitarist. I walk to the section of the store where Glenn's CDs can be found and leaf through the various albums. His band is called Glenn Lumb & The Independence and their album art work is very Americanised—a sprawling dessert adorns the front of one; an eagle in flight with red, white and blue feathers fills another. When the queue has diminished, I watch as Glenn stands up, shaking the hand he has been using to write with, and walks towards us.

'We doing this, then?' he asks.

GLENN CARRIES THREE coffees towards our table and I can't make up my mind what to think of him. His fringe, cut straight across his forehead, and his green parka suggest that he is trying to keep hold of those heady days in the 90s. The rise of Britpop. Though, the snakeskin cowboy boots and the red spotty neckerchief are at odds with the rest of his look, intimating some sort of transatlantic whim. He's wearing Aviator style sunglasses despite the indoor coffee shop setting.

'Here you go,' he says, as he pushes the coffees in our direction and slides into the booth with us. He takes the top off his takeaway cup and pours in a number of sugars, blowing on the steaming liquid before replacing the lid.

'I imagine this is about Duane?' he says. 'I saw the press conference yesterday.'

I nod. 'We have been led to believe you saw him on the night of the murder, in Havana.'

'I did indeed. Known him for years, though I've not been a customer in a long time.' He holds his arm up and shows us a tattoo of a tally on his wrist. 'Three years clean now. I get it updated every year. Keeps me on the straight and narrow.'

'So, your relationship with Duane is…'

'Strictly friendship,' he confirms. 'I know it sounds odd—a recovering addict hanging out with a dealer, but it's not like I see him often. We don't arrange to hang out or anything like that, I just see him about town, out and about like.'

'And did you arrange to meet him at Havana last night?'

'Nope. Like I say, we don't do that. I was there, he was there, we hung out. But not by prior arrangement.'

'Did you leave together?' Andy asks.

'Definitely not. If we left together, it'd be to go back to his, and going back to his would mean dancing with the devil—all that coke lying about. No, I had a few orange juices and left.'

'Could anyone verify this?'

'Divorced twice,' he says, holding up his hand to show no wedding ring. 'So no, I didn't go home to anyone. And no one would shag me, despite my best efforts, so I went home very much alone. I bet the CCTV could show it though. They have a camera everywhere in that place.'

'We're in the process of getting the footage,' I say.

From out of the corner of my eye, I notice two teenagers, probably about fifteen or sixteen years old. They are both wearing T-shirts adorned with Morrissey's face and are casting furtive glances our way and whispering excitedly. One of them gets up, the other follows, and they make their way to our table.

'Excuse me, but is it really you?' the one with the feeble beginnings of a moustache says.

'It's really me,' Glenn confirms.

'Would you mind if we have a picture with you?' the other boy stutters, phone already in hand.

Glenn puffs out his chest and raises his eyebrows smugly at Andy and me. He poses for a photo and gives each boy a friendly pat on the back as they exchange pleasantries.

'Sorry about that,' he says as he sits back down. 'Occupational hazard.'

As they are walking away, one of the boys raises his phone to his ear and declares to whoever is on the other end that they have just met Johnny Marr. Glenn chuckles to himself, deflating slightly. I decide that I like this man.

'At least I made their day,' he says. 'Even if I'm not who they thought I was. Anyway, where were we?'

'We were discussing Duane Miller,' Andy says, getting back on track. 'Was he still there when you left?'

Glenn nods. 'He was with his friends. They were just about to make their move on a group of girls and there is nothing more tragic than watching that happen when you're sober. That's when I headed off.'

'Did you say goodbye to him?'

'No,' he says, shaking his head. 'He was in the zone. You don't mess with the zone.'

'Was Johnny there?'

'Mayhem? Nah, man. If he's there, I usually split.'

'Why?'

'Because I still haven't forgiven that fucker for leaving the band, our band, on the upward curve. Look, I'm very lucky that I still get to do this for a living. But, I'm playing half empty rooms built for a thousand, maximum, when I should've been playing in arenas. He took that opportunity away from me, and I haven't, nor will I ever, forgive him.'

'Why did he leave the band?' I ask, keen to get inside access to the man we are hunting for.

'For her. Amanda. He'd made his money—endorsements, television appearances and what have you. Everyone wants the front man. To be honest, I felt like that for a while too. I was honoured to be in his band. He had star potential and he fulfilled it. I never fully have and it eats at me every day.'

'Did you enjoy being in a band with him?' says Andy.

'Yeah. He was a control freak. He'd write guitar parts for me and show me how I should play them. Like I said, I felt lucky to be riding his coattails at the start, so I was happy to do what he said. But, by the end of the band, it was exhausting. He'd keep us waiting at photoshoots, recording sessions would get cancelled because he was on a bender or some bullshit. That's why I called my band The Independence. I'm free now to do what I want.'

He takes off his sunglasses and rubs his eyes wearily. He pulls up the sleeve of his parka and checks the time on his watch.

'Sorry about this, but I've got to be at soundcheck in the next hour, so I have to go,' he says.

We all stand up, thank him for his time and just before he turns to go, he invites us to his gig tonight, saying he'll put us on the guestlist. We thank him and tell him that we will see him later.

10

I SIT AT the kitchen table and pause the video. The manager of the club, Tony, was true to his word and had sent across the CCTV footage from his club quite quickly. The video starts from an hour before doors open to the punters and finishes at just after five in the morning. I'd watched the employees go about their work on double speed; watched as they'd made sure the VIP areas were spick and span, the fridges were fully stocked and the bottles of expensive champagne were displayed prominently and invitingly. When the doors were opened, I'd slowed the video down to normal speed and studied each face as they passed by the entrance table; some paying, some not. The easy way to tell who was held in high regard. The old adage of "become rich and you don't have to pay for anything."

Now, as Duane enters with a group of friends, I pause it. I take a screen shot and paste the photo into an e-mail, sending it to the station in the hope that his friends will be identifiable. One of them might have been the caller who alerted us to Duane's body in the first place. Once the email has been sent, I hit play on the video and watch as he and his friends stop at the table. The friends all hand the woman a note, though Duane doesn't. When all hands have been stamped, Duane waltzes towards the bar, his friends in tow.

I check my watch and know that if I don't get a move on, we're going to be late for the gig, so I pause the footage and close my laptop.

In the living room, Tom and my dad are chatting animatedly about football while Leo chomps on a rice cake and gurgles happily.

'Ready?' I ask, bending down to pick Leo up. He nuzzles his head into my shoulder, coating the outside of my jacket in crumbs and saliva. Tom nods, grabs his coat and jumps up. He kisses the top of Leo's fluffy head and goes to find the keys. I hand Leo to dad.

'Spare keys are in the kitchen. Leo's milk is in the fridge and if you need me at any stage…'

'I won't,' he interrupts. 'It's been ages since you two got any time together. So, go. Enjoy yourselves. We'll be just fine.'

He descends into baby language as he addresses Leo, smacking his lips on the baby's bare tummy, causing him to chuckle heartily and squirm to get away. I give them once last wave and leave the house. Tom has started the car so when I get in, it's already on its way to warming up. We drive towards the city centre venue, commenting on how strange it is to be alone.

Tom finds a car parking space close to the Apollo, an ugly Grade II listed building, and we make our way to the end of the line. I zip my jacket up to my chin and reach into my bag, pulling out my phone so that I can text dad to see if everything is okay. Waiting for me, though, is a message from the man himself.

Don't even consider texting me. WE WILL BE FINE. I've done this before, and look at how well you turned out… well, actually don't use that as an example! Have a great night. Love, Dad.

Content, I slip my phone back into my bag as the line starts to shuffle forward and we make it to the door just as a downpour starts; the heavy rainfall causing an uproarious reaction to the ticket holders waiting behind us. My bag is checked by an uninterested security guard, who has a cursory glance inside before admitting us entry. I have the urge to bust his balls about the lax check, but Tom notices my expression just in time, puts an arm around me and edges me away from him.

We find our seats just as the lights dim and the opening notes of Dancing in the Dark by Bruce Springsteen ring out, prompting a huge cheer from the crowd. Glenn Lumb and his band stride from the side of the stage and take their places, letting The Boss finish the first chorus, before the music fades and Glenn addresses the crowd.

'I am Glenn Lumb and we are The Independence,' he says, before the drummer clicks his sticks together and the band launch into their first song. It's not to my taste, but Tom seems to like it. He's nodding his head and tapping his foot. I last a few songs, which all sound the same to me, before I've had enough. I take Tom's drink request and make my way down the steps towards the bar.

The bar area is not in keeping with the tasteful décor in other areas of the building. Neon signs have been drilled into the ancient brickwork and bright blue tables have been set up. Everything looks gaudy and so out of place.

The bar is full of people uninterested in the support band, preferring instead to talk to friends whilst waiting for the main act to take to the stage. At six quid per pint, I think I would've stayed at home a while longer than pay through the nose for the watered-down lager that's served here, though, that could be me showing my age. I join the back of one of the queues and wait to be served.

After what feels like an eternity, I am next in line. The man in front of me orders and I watch on as the harried barman sets a plastic pint cup under one of the taps and flicks it on, letting the lager pour whilst he makes his way to the fridge to retrieve a bottle of cider, trying to avoid the other employees who are running around like headless chickens too. He flicks the tap off, takes payment and switches his gaze to me without so much as a thank you. As I take a step forward, a blaze of erratic action out of the corner of my eye makes me flinch and a sharp gasp escapes my lips as my chest is suddenly doused in cold liquid.

The man who was in front of me in the queue has dropped both his drinks, the remainder of the pint that hasn't been spilled over my blouse is currently soaking into the plush red carpet. He repeats apology after apology and reaches for some napkins from the bar, and dabs my left breast before he realises what he's done. When he notices that he is currently rubbing the boob of a woman he doesn't know, he drops the napkin and holds up both hands, his apologies getting louder. I laugh at the ridiculousness of the last five seconds and leave the queue, walking to the end of the bar. I grab a handful of napkins and take a seat at a table, dabbing them onto my top.

The red-faced man walks over sheepishly and stands beside me.

'I'm so sorry. I tripped over my shoelace,' he says. 'I can assure you I'm not a sex pest, I was just trying to help.'

'Don't worry about it,' I laugh. 'These things happen. Most of it went on the floor anyway.'

'Let me buy you a drink to apologise.'

'It's okay,' I say. 'I need to get one for my boyfriend anyway.'

'I'll get that too. My girlfriend is waiting on me inside so I need to get more drinks anyway.'

I thank him, tell him what I want and a few minutes later, he returns with four drinks in a cardboard holder. He sets my two cups on the table, sits down beside me and checks if I'm okay.

It's the first time I get a proper look at him. The first thing I notice are his eyes; icy blue and framed by the longest eyelashes I've ever seen. His dark hair is shaved at the side and longer on top and a week of growth covers his chiselled jawline. He could be mistaken for a model, if it weren't for what he is wearing. A Captain America T-shirt has been pulled over a long sleeve T-shirt, recalling a fad from the mid-2000s. Dirty tennis shoes protrude from under bootcut jeans.

'I feel terrible,' he says. 'I really can't apologise enough.'

'Please, don't worry. Like I said, these things happen.'

I stand up and he follows suit.

'Well,' I say, 'thank you for the drinks, you really didn't need to.'

'Thanks for being so understanding. I'm Eli, by the way.'

'Erika,' I reply. 'Well, I best be getting back to my seat.'

'You're lucky to have got seats. I find that now that I'm past thirty, standing at these things wreaks havoc with my back! Have a good night.'

He smiles and once again I'm struck by those blue eyes. I compose myself, smile and walk back towards the stairs, drinks in hand. As I sit down, Glenn announces from the stage that they're about to play their last song of the evening and thanks the crowd for coming in early. They play their final song and leave the stage to lukewarm applause and cheers.

I can see why he was so angry at Johnny Mayhem earlier. To go from being in one of the biggest bands in the country and having the world at your feet, to being a support act that no one gives a shit about for an up-and-coming band in a mid-sized venue must sting somewhat.

The lights go up again and Tom enquires about my top. I tell him the story of Eli spilling his beer and attempting to wipe me down. Tom howls with laughter and I join in. Though things have been tense at home, what with baby tiredness and the pressures that come from being a parent alongside my testing employment situation, the warm feeling that everything will work out alright settles into my stomach.

The remainder of the night passes in a swirl of music and lights. The main act, a five piece from Stockport, are clearly on their way to the big-time. Their music is fresh and it's easy to see that they are loving every minute of being on stage.

Truthfully, I'm glad when it's all over and as we make our way through our front door, the fatigue hits me. Dad is snoozing on the sofa and Leo is out for the count in his cot, wrapped up in his colourful blanket. I brush my teeth and make my way to the bedroom, where I fall asleep in record time.

11

ONCE LEO HAS had his morning milk and is happily napping, I sit at the kitchen table and open the lid of my laptop. The CCTV file is already open, paused at the same place I'd stopped watching last night.

The footage resumes with Duane and his group of friends ordering drinks at the bar. They stand in a semi-circle and watch the barman pour pint after pint. When six drinks have been lined up on the bar, Duane reaches into his pocket and pulls out a wad of money, handing a few notes across the bar and exchanging words with the worker. Probably telling him to keep the change, as the barman doesn't return to the group again.

Each of the men in the group grabs a drink off the bar, before walking to the back of the room, near to the VIP booths. They occupy the space, dancing stiffly to the music and checking out the women with leering stares. A tall woman with a pixie cut moves towards the group, holding a tray of shot glasses. She and Duane converse for a minute, before she stalks off out of shot, an annoyed look etched on her face.

The pattern continues for most of the night; drink, dance, ogle. Eventually, they make their way into the middle of the dancefloor and try to ingratiate themselves with a group of women. Duane seems the most willing to make a fool of himself. Perhaps it's liquid confidence or maybe it's just his personality, but he is the one making all the moves. He's pulling out dance moves I thought disappeared with the 90s. But, to be fair to him, they seem to be working. The circle of women opens up and the men close in. It's hard to see detail, but they all seem like cool, hip young people. Not my scene at all.

A while later, when the group of men have made themselves at home in a booth at the side of the room, Glenn enters the frame. He is walking past the table when he stops suddenly, as if someone has shouted his name. He turns to the table and greets Duane with an elaborate handshake. He points to the back of the room, leaves the video and returns shortly after. I assume he has been to the toilet. When he returns to the table, he talks to Duane for a short while. It all looks friendly enough and then Glenn leaves. The two do not interact again for the duration of the video. Duane leaves with his group of friends at around one thirty and the girls they were dancing with leave at just after two o'clock.

I close the laptop with more questions than answers. I knew before watching that Johnny had not been there, but part of me had expected him to be in the video, disguised, leering from a corner of the darkened room, Scooby-Doo style.

So, how did Johnny get into Duane's house? Was he waiting for him outside the club? Did he drive him home? Or, was he waiting on Duane's doorstep under the guise of a late-night drug deal?

I send an e-mail requesting CCTV from the exterior of the club and as much footage as we can get from around Duane's neck of the woods. Reports from the officers keeping vigil outside Johnny's house suggest that he only has the one car, and it's a pretty recognisable one at that, so if it were to show up on CCTV, it'd be easy to track.

I phone Andy to make sure he is still okay to meet me at Johnny's house in an hour's time. A search warrant has been obtained. Reports suggest he has not been home since the night of the murder—an unmarked police car has been stationed outside constantly since shortly after Duane's body was discovered. The neighbours haven't seen him for a few days either, though they suggested there was nothing unusual in that. Even if he hasn't been there, I'm hoping that something he has left behind will move the investigation along. Something to do with Duane, or a clue as to where he might be hiding.

I close the laptop and walk to the bedroom to wake Tom up. He looks at me with bleary eyes, despite it being nearly ten o'clock. I get in the shower, wash away the weariness of the previous late night and get ready for the day. When I enter the kitchen, Tom is sitting with his head on the table, a cup of black coffee in his hand. Hangover plus children is a bad combination. I kiss him on the top of the head, blow Leo a kiss from afar so as not to disturb his naptime and head for the door. I get in the car, program Johnny's address into the sat nav and set sail towards Ashton-under-Lyne.

WALKING INTO THE rock star's house is like taking an involuntary trip back in time. As soon as my foot touches the welcome mat, I'm transported back, seven years ago, to the night Amanda's body was discovered. Not much has changed. The walls are the same colour and the framed prints hanging on the stairs remain the same too. I thought perhaps a family member or a friend might've moved in during the time that Johnny was in prison, but the house feels like a shell; unlived-in.

Andy and I split up. He ascends the stairs while I remain downstairs, on the agreement that if anything of note is found, we call each other straight away.

I make my way through the house, though there is nothing that catches my eye. The living room is orderly. An acoustic guitar rests on a stand in the corner of the room. The cushions on the sofa are plump and crease-free and a thick layer of dust coats most of the surfaces in the room. Despite Johnny having been released from prison over three months ago, the room appears unused. I wonder did he return here at all when he walked free.

My answer to that question is in the kitchen. When I open the door, I'm greeted by the smell of rot. I open the bin to find it almost filled to the top, though it is not the source of the putrid smell. I follow my nose to the large, American-style fridge and almost vomit when I pull the handle. Inside, there are several plastic boxes of meat. The 'use by' date is over a week ago. I close the fridge and walk out of the room, in order to gulp fresh air into my lungs, just as Andy comes down the stairs.

'Nothing out of the ordinary,' he says. 'Johnny seemed to be a bit of neat freak. All his clothes are hung up and there doesn't seem to be any missing. His toothbrush and toiletries are all there too.'

'Any sign of his wallet?'

He shakes his head. 'What you thinking?'

'I'm thinking that Johnny's argument with Duane and his disappearance are linked. Part of me thinks that he didn't come home from the club that night; that he's hiding in some safe house or flat he owns that we don't know about. He killed Duane, I'm sure of that. And I'm still sure he killed his wife, no matter what bullshit evidence got him out of jail.'

'So, what next?' asks Andy.

'Firstly, I want his bank cards traced. If he didn't come back here after the club that night, I reckon he's bought supplies; clothes, food and whatnot. Secondly, we need to find out if he has any properties that aren't listed to him. We know he hasn't been here, so, where is he? I'm going to get back to Tony and ask for the CCTV from the night Duane and Johnny argued. That might tell us something. We might be able to track his movements when he left the club. I'll ask Ross to get on that. The man has an encyclopaedic knowledge of the CCTV cameras in the city.'

My phone buzzes in my pocket.

'Hello?' I answer.

'Erika, we've got one of Duane's friends in an interview room. He came in under his own steam, says he wants to help. If you're busy, I can get someone else to interview…'

'No,' I interrupt. 'I'll be there shortly. I want to hear what he has to say myself. Thank you.'

I hang up the phone and tell Andy we are leaving. We walk out of the house and approach the lone car in the driveway, which Andy stops to admire. The shining blue paint job, the sloping headlights and the angled mesh grill make the car appear like it's breaking the speed limit even when at a standstill. I look at it with disdain. Why anyone would buy a car that costs more than some houses and can reach a top speed that is nearly triple that of the motorway speed limit is beyond me.

Making up for a having a small cock is my closest guess.

Andy bends down to look in the windows, but finds that they are too tinted to see through. He rests his head on the glass and I follow suit on the other side, just about making out some details of the leather clad interior of the two-seater. There are a few CD cases on the passenger side seat and a bottle of water lying unopened in the footwell.

'Jesus,' Andy says. 'Oh, to be rich and famous.'

'I prefer your Clio,' I say to much laughter, as we make our way down the sloped driveway. As we walk out the gate, I look up the street and spot the unmarked police car. I give a quick wave and get one in return from the officer in the passenger seat. My heart goes out to them. When they joined the police, they probably didn't anticipate that they'd be paid to sit in the cramped confines of a car for shifts on end, keeping watch on an empty house. However, when under pressure, people can do stupid things, and returning to a safe place can be one of those. For all the boredom these officers are going through, they could be the ones to catch the killer.

I get in the passenger side of our own car. Andy fires up the engine and we head back to the station.

I ENTER THE interview room with Andy at my side and give the man on the opposite side of the table a smile that is meant to relax him. It doesn't work, and he doesn't return it. Instead, he looks around the room nervously, avoiding our eyes. Andy and I sit down. I reassure the man that he is doing the right thing by being here, though he doesn't seem convinced. He pulls off his baseball cap and runs his hands through his thick, wavy hair. I press record on the console and begin the interview.

'Beginning interview with…'

'Lucas Young,' he mutters.

'Present are DI Erika Piper and DS Andy Robinson,' I continue. 'Lucas is here of his own free will. He is free to leave at any time.'

I give him another smile.

'So, Lucas, why *are* you here?'

'No one can know that I am, yeah?' he says. 'I ain't no grass, but I want to do right by my boy, Duane, so here I am.'

'And you're absolutely doing the right thing. Any information we can get is gratefully received. So, what can you tell us?'

'It was a normal night out. We had drinks at Duane's beforehand, went to the club together and left together.'

'Are you referring to the night of the 27th September? The night Duane died?'

Lucas confirms that he is.

'Did you go back to his house?'

'Nah, we all got taxis to our own houses. I shared with Huey and Bricky. Colly got one on his own and so did Duane.'

'Did you all leave at the same time?'

'Everyone except for Duane,' he nods. 'He went to the Spar across the road from the taxi rank to get a few bits. One of our friends went round to his place in the morning to pick him up for five-a-side, and found his body.'

'Which friend?'

'I don't want to say,' he says, looking down at the table.

'If you do tell us, it may help with the investigation. Any information they have about the scene of the crime could be very beneficial.'

I watch as his fingers trace along the edges of the rounded plastic corners of the table. He looks like he is in danger of shutting down, so I decide to move on.

'Okay. Did anything happen that was out of the ordinary?'

He shakes his head. 'Nope. Same as usual. We had a few drinks, we tried it on with a couple of girls but there wasn't much doing, so we left.'

I can feel the frustration buzzing inside me. This feels like a waste of time. I reach across to the stop button to end the interview, but he stops me.

'I wanted to tell you about something that happened last week though. We were all at the club when Johnny Mayhem came in. You know it was Duane's evidence that freed him? We thought he'd be over the moon—free at last for something he didn't do. But he didn't seem happy. It was the first time they'd been in the same room since he got out of jail and we thought he'd treat us all to bottles of champagne to say thank you.'

'But, he didn't?' says Andy.

'Nah, man. He came marching up to our group, swaying already and it was just past ten o'clock. Duane looked pleased and held out his hand. Johnny came up, ignored his hand and whispered something in Duane's ear. Duane shook his head. Johnny laughed in his face and pushed him. Duane got up close and whispered something back. Johnny shoved him in the chest again, harder this time, before the bouncers got involved. We were going to leave, but Johnny wriggled free and staggered away from us and out the door.'

'Did Duane tell you what Johnny had said?'

'Yeah. He wanted to buy heroin from Duane, but he refused. He told Johnny that he wouldn't be dealing to him anymore and that he should use this time to keep clean. That's when Johnny shoved him.'

He holds his hands up to show us that that is all he knows. I end the recording, and thank him for the information. He replaces the baseball cap, pulls it low over his eyes, places his thrumming headphones into his ears and leaves the interview room with Andy. I walk across to my office and take a seat behind my desk, thinking about what I've just learned.

Johnny and Duane's argument had been about drugs. About the drug dealer refusing to ply the rock star with his wares. That showed that Duane was either a bad businessman or had a huge heart.

Is that why Johnny murdered him? Simply because he'd refused to deal to him? Or was there something else?

He'd implied on the documentary that he was pissed off with Duane for waiting for so long to use the evidence he had to free him from jail. Maybe it was a mixture of the two reasons. Whatever the reason, it changes nothing. Johnny Mayhem is our man. We just need to find him.

12

I KNOCK ON Susie's door and, after a few minutes, she answers with a gurgling Adam in her arms.

'Thanks so much for the text,' I say, following her in to the living room. 'I hadn't realised I'd forgotten Leo's blanket when we were at the café.'

She waves a hand in my direction, as if to say don't mention it, before retrieving the forgotten blanket from a pine sideboard. I fold it into a small square and push it into my bag, before sitting on the floor beside her smiling baby as he moves a car back and forth. He giggles with glee at the attention he's getting and reaches for a book that he likes, which I read to him, doing the actions that the text requires of me. Again, he howls with laughter and attempts to copy the actions.

'Do you mind if I use the toilet?' I ask Susie.

'Not at all,' she replies.

I push myself off the floor and start for the door. As I'm about to turn left into the kitchen, she calls after me.

'Oh sorry, you'll need to go upstairs, the downstairs one is out of action.'

I follow her advice and make my way up the stairs. Having relieved myself and washed my hands, I make my way to the living room again to find Susie slumped in the armchair, her eyelids fluttering. When I enter the room, she shakes her head and climbs into a sitting position.

'You okay?' I ask.

'Yeah,' she answers, rubbing her eyes with the back of her hands. 'He's just not sleeping well at the minute, so neither am I.'

She points to a bottle of Night Nurse on the sideboard.

'I've been having that during the nights he stays at his dad's. I thought I'd sleep like a log on the nights he is away, but I sleep worse if anything. I've started taking the sleeping potion and it's helping a bit.'

'If only they made Night Nurse for babies, they'd make a fortune!' I laugh. 'If you ever want an afternoon to yourself, I'd be glad to have Adam if I'm not working.'

She stands up and hugs me, thanks me for my kind offer and reciprocates. It makes me feel glad that we signed up for those NCT classes all those months ago.

My phone buzzes in my pocket and when I answer, it's Andy, telling me that the CCTV from the club of the night Johnny and Duane clashed is in, as well as another interesting development.

I hang up and promise Susie that we will get together again soon. She thanks me again for my offer of childcare and walks me to the front door. She watches me as I turn the car around and waves me down the driveway.

I GET OUT of the lift on the third floor and find Andy in the staff room, making a cup of coffee. He pulls another mug from the cupboard and throws a teabag in at my request. Drinks made, we make our way to my office. I turn the computer on and sit in my chair, setting my tea on the side.

'What's this new development then?' I ask.

Andy sets his mug of coffee on my desk.

'The cell site stuff came back from Johnny's phone. It's interesting. He got a number of messages throughout the evening. They pinged a mast near his home in Ashton, and we know he wasn't at the club on the night of Duane's death, so it seems he was there most of the night. The next time it pinged, at around ten past three in the morning, it was from a mast near to Duane's house. So, using this, we can place him at the scene.'

'Can we use it to trace where he is right now?' I ask, the words tumbling out like a torrent.

'The techie lads tried that already. Apparently, there were no more pings after the one at Duane's. They reckon the message he got probably pushed him into removing his SIM card and destroying the phone. It's common knowledge that we can track movement by phone and, with what he had just been up to, they think he probably realised that we could pinpoint his location to there, so he got rid before travelling onwards.'

The momentary glimmer of hope abandons me. It would've been too easy; too good to be true. I thank Andy for the update and tell him to keep me in the loop, on the very off chance that his phone turns on again. He tells me that he will, before leaving me in peace with my CCTV footage.

I access my emails and locate the footage that has been sent across from the night Duane and Johnny had their face off. It leaps into life with a double click of my mouse. The video is shorter this time, and doesn't show the setting up before doors open. Instead, Duane and his buddies are front and centre, already in their apparent favoured spot by the back of the club, drinks in hand.

The dancefloor is busy and Duane's eyes rove it, probably searching for the lucky lady he plans on wooing. One of the group heads in the direction of the toilet, while Duane ventures to the bar, both returning again a few minutes later. They talk amongst themselves before taking a few steps towards the dancefloor. Duane stops dead, his eyes bulging as if he has just seen a ghost off screen. His body language changes from group leader alpha male to concerned little boy.

A skeletal Johnny Mayhem strides into view, his short hair accentuating his chiselled jaw. Duane extends a hand, which Johnny ignores. They talk animatedly for a minute, before Johnny leans in and whispers in the drug dealer's ear. Duane shakes his head and Johnny shoves him in the chest with both hands. The group close in around Johnny, the nervous energy easy to see, even in black and white. It feels like the moment before a bomb goes off. On the screen, Duane holds up his hands to pacify them. They sink back half a step, prepared to jump in again if needed.

By now, the motion of the dancefloor has stopped and everyone in the vicinity is watching the unfolding events with varying expressions. Some look worried, while others look positively delighted at the possibility of some kind of drama. Nearly everyone in the place has a camera phone pointed at the confrontation.

Johnny and Duane are so embroiled in their own world that they don't seem to have noticed. It's Duane's turn to whisper in Johnny's ear, though the result is the same. He gets a two-handed shove in the chest. Harder this time.

So far, the action has played out exactly how Duane's friend had described it in the interview.

As violence threatens to explode, the vampire-esque manager runs towards them, though is beaten by the slender frame of Glenn Lumb. The guitarist gets between Johnny and Duane and barks orders. Johnny lunges at Glenn and grabs him by the throat, but Glenn quickly shrugs him off, his eyes wild with anger. There is some finger pointing and posturing between Duane's group and The Darling Roses' singer, but in the end, he holds his hands up and walks away from the group and out of shot.

Glenn exchanges words with Duane before striding purposefully out of shot, following Johnny's path. The footage ends a few seconds later.

I think back to my conversation with Glenn in the coffee shop. He hadn't mentioned having any kind of altercation with Johnny, and I make a note to follow up what happened after the footage ends.

I rewind it to the start. This time, I keep my eyes on the gawking onlookers, in the hope that something stands out. A few B-list celebrity faces I sort of recognise mill about, but aside from that, no one stands out. The action unfolds as before, though this time, someone else catches my eye.

It's a shot girl with a blonde bob. She watches Johnny grab Glenn from the crowd, though she has positioned herself perfectly to get the best view. As Johnny stalks off and Glenn and Duane talk, she sets her drinks tray down on a nearby table and follows in Johnny's wake. A group of lads push and pull at each other excitedly, and knock into her, causing her wig to fall onto the floor, exposing a dark pixie-cut. She grabs the wig and exits the video seconds before Glenn does.

I scribble another note.

Who is the mystery brunette?

I find Glenn's details and pick up the phone, dialling the number he gave me. It rings out, with no option to leave a voicemail. I open a new internet browser window and find his band's website. Glenn and The Independence are currently in mainland Europe, playing as support act for The Honeydews. I make a note of the date the tour finishes so that I can follow up the lead with him when he gets back.

I pick up the receiver again, this time phoning Havana, in the hope that Tony is in.

A woman answers, telling me that Tony is not currently there, and asks if she can help. I describe the brunette shot-seller from the CCTV footage and ask if she knows anything about her.

'It sounds like Bea,' she says.

'Pixie-cut?'

'Some days, yeah. She likes to change up her looks with a wig. Ginger, one night, blonde the next. She's been working here part time for years. She started when she was young. Tony has tried to promote her to management a few times, but she insists she's happy doing what she's doing.'

'Why do you think that is?' I ask, incredulous that's she'd pass up a job with marginally more responsibility for a whole lot more money.

'She likes being out in the crowd, flirting with whatever celeb is in that night. Have you seen her body? All she has to do is shake that booty and the boys come running. She also makes a shitload in tips, so there's that too.'

A thought occurs to me.

'Do you think she has had any contact with Johnny Mayhem?'

'I doubt it,' she says. 'I think she started while Mayhem was in prison. He did come here almost every night since he was released though, so there's a chance she could've. Do you want me to get her to call you?'

'That'd be great,' I reply, before ending the call.

13

I FLICK THROUGH the pages again, waiting for any detail at all to jump out at me. So far, nothing has.

It feels like the millionth time I've looked through the case notes from the murder of Amanda Mayhem. It is more than likely a time-consuming, fruitless exercise, but if one detail from this helps with the current case and the hunt for Johnny, it will feel like time well spent.

As the frustration begins to spill over, I push the folder away from me and stand up, moving out from behind my desk to pace the office. Sometimes, letting the mind wander leads to some small nugget of information rearing its head in the subconsciousness. I try to shut out the whirr of the computer and the chatter from the shared space outside my door, but to no avail. Nothing is forthcoming.

I walk back around the desk and throw myself into my chair. I pull my mobile from my bag and search through the contacts list. When I reach Simon Black, I stop, hovering over the dial button.

Simon Black had been the DI; my superior, when we entered Johnny Mayhem's house. It was on his orders that Mayhem was arrested for the murder of his wife that night. Shortly after, Simon quit. He couldn't handle the media scrutiny and the pressure of the case; the constant meetings and the *"my dick is bigger than yours"* attitude the DCI at the time had had.

I wonder how he will react to being dragged back into the past.

Only one way to find out.

I press the green call button and listen as the phone rings. Just as I think it is going to answerphone, a deep voice answers.

'I had a feeling I'd be hearing from you.' The gruffness of the voice can't hide the smile behind it. 'I assume this isn't a social call?'

'Not exactly,' I reply. 'I've got a few things I'd like to run by you. Are you free?'

'Not at the minute. I'm at work. How about a beer tonight? You're buying.'

We arrange to meet at a bar near his house later before hanging up. I'm hopeful that, as the more experienced police officer at the time, some small nugget of information may have stuck in his mind, however insignificant it may have seemed at the time. Cases can be solved on such little bits of luck.

THE SIMON BLACK of a decade ago would look painfully out of place sitting in a bar like this. The distressed walls, worn stone floor and minimal dressing of the long, narrow room are a far cry from the sticky-carpeted boozers of yesteryear.

Simon sits near the back of the room, a scented candle burning in the centre of the table, lighting his face like a character from a horror film. He glances up when he sees me approaching. He taps a few buttons on his phone, shoves it back in his pocket and stands up to greet me with a hug. Not much about him has changed in the years since I last saw him. His thick head of hair is still a very natural brown. His goatee is well trimmed and maintained and his eyes still sparkle with a certain type of mischief. I throw my bag onto the vacant chair and take his drink order, before walking to the bar.

A bored looking barman in a waistcoat sets down a glass he was cleaning and dawdles over to me. He takes my drink order and begins pouring the first pint, slashing at the head with a metal scraper before setting it on the bar in front of me. He repeats the process and I pay for the drinks, walking back to the table with a glass in each hand.

'£12.60 for two fucking drinks!' I say, sliding the pint across the table, careful not to spill a drop.

He laughs, masking a hint of embarrassment. He scoops up his pint and takes a long pull on it, a contented sigh escaping his lips as he sets it back on the table.

'Is this your usual haunt then?' I ask. 'There isn't even a pool table!'

'No,' he laughs. 'I've never been here before. I'm meeting someone later on, and thought I'd try somewhere nice. TripAdvisor gave it great reviews.'

'Is it a date?'

He nods his head, and takes another tactical drink in order to give himself a bit of thinking time.

'First date?'

'I thought you wanted to talk about the case?' he says, light-hearted.

'Well, I do. But this is just as juicy. Let me get this out of my system first and then we'll talk shop.'

'Fine,' he sighs. 'First date. Met her online. We've been talking for about a week. She seems nice. Her name is Rebecca. Happy?'

'Delighted,' I say.

Simon Black had always been unlucky in love. He'd never married, never really had a serious relationship as far as I knew. I was pleased to see him embracing modern technology in the search for someone special. I refrain from any more questions.

'So, what did you actually want to talk about?' he says.

I push the files from Amanda Mayhem's murder investigation across the table towards him. He picks them up with a knowing nod and glances inside.

'You know, I haven't seen the files in nearly seven years, but every fucking word is embossed on my brain. And I reckon they are for you, too. Is something bothering you?' he asks.

I sigh. 'That's the thing. Not really. And it should. The evidence gathered at the time was watertight. So, what am I missing here?'

He takes a perfunctory look through the files, more for my sake than his.

'You're not missing anything,' he says. 'Everything pointed to Johnny Mayhem. There was no forced entry. There'd been rumours about her playing away from home in the papers for months. He was sitting on the bed with the fucking murder weapon in his hands, covered in her blood. The murder weapon that only had his and Amanda's prints on it.'

'So, you still believe it was him?' I ask. 'Despite what the judge says.'

'Course I do. We were there. You and me. We saw him. That look on his face. It was him, no doubt about it. And I reckon it was him that killed that drug dealer too.'

'You do?'

'Did you see the documentary? He pretty much came out and said that he'd be seeking some sort of revenge. A few months later, the guy is dead.'

'And he left a rose at the scene, like he did with Amanda. Though, we've managed to keep that from the press, so that's between you and me.'

'I assume you have a team checking in with every florist in the land?'

'The land? Do you remember police budgets? We've teams working through Manchester, to start with. If we need to expand, we will.'

With nothing else to learn from him, we slip into an easy conversation about how his life has changed since he gave up policing, my new family and everything in between. He's easy to talk to, and the evening ends with a hug and promises to make this a more regular thing.

'Good luck for your date,' I say, as I wrap a scarf around my neck. 'Do you think she's the one?'

'She'd better be, now that I've seen the price of the drinks here,' he laughs.

A FEW HOURS later, I climb into bed, our meeting still fresh in my head. Frustrated though I am about the lack of clues as to where Johnny Mayhem might be, or who he might be with, I'm positive we are on the right track. He'll have to surface sooner or later.

I pick up my phone and type a text message to Simon, thanking him for tonight and telling him how lovely it was to see him. I plug the charger into the base of my phone and roll over, cuddling tight into Tom's back.

A vibration rouses me from the slumber I was falling into. I roll over again and pick up my phone, seeing that I've received a reply from Simon. I open it, expecting it to be a quick goodnight message in return, but when I open it, I let out a cry. Tom jerks awake and asks me if I'm okay.

I can't move. I'm transfixed by what is on the screen.

A picture of Simon Black's body, laying in the doorway of his home. His face is unrecognisable and covered in blood.

A lavender rose rests in the open palm of his right hand.

14

THE HOUSES IN the normally peaceful, quiet cul-de-sac flash blue in time with the police car lights. Despite the hour and the lashing rain, the excitement of a heavy police presence and a hastily erected forensic tent has tempted the nosier residents out onto the street. A harassed looking officer stands just inside the taped off crime scene, tasked with keeping the crowd at bay.

I pull into the street and park my car in a driveway near to Simon's house. Making my way through the crowd, I duck under the tape and sign the log book, before suiting up. I make my way to the tent erected against the front wall of the house. I steel myself, knowing full well what is waiting for me just inside. I take a deep breath, pull the flap open and move inside.

John Kirrane and the crime scene photographer are deep in conversation. The forensic pathologist acknowledges me with a raise of his index finger, but otherwise, remains attentive, listening to what the man wielding the camera has to say. When their discussion is done and a number of photographs have been taken, John turns to me.

'I'm sorry, Erika. I know he was your friend, but this isn't pretty. Are you sure you want to see?'

I nod, and he moves out of the way, revealing the scene.

The front door of Simon's house is open, light and heat spilling out into the night from the hallway. Simon's body lies flat on the floor; mostly inside, though his feet rest on the step outside. He is still wearing the smart clothes he had been in earlier, though the pocket square that had been nestled nicely in the top pocket of his blazer is gone and his crisp white shirt is covered in blood.

The source of the blood is obvious.

His face shows the signs of untold violence.

He has either been hit so hard or so many times that the features are difficult to make out. His nose has been flattened, a thin ridge hinting at where it once was. Split lips are parted, showing that every tooth has been broken, leaving a black hole of pain. The eyes sockets are smashed to bits and are already a violent purple, despite the attack not happening long ago.

I force my eyes to leave his face to scan the rest of the body. There doesn't seem to be any damage done elsewhere.

'It would've been quick,' John says, kindly.

'Baseball bat?' I ask.

'You know I never like to give anything away after a quick assessment, but, between you and me, yes, I think so. The blunt force trauma injuries are consistent with a number of strikes from an object such as a baseball bat.'

I glance at the purple rose in his hand.

The calling card of Johnny Mayhem.

'Has the house been secured?' I ask.

'Yes,' he nods. 'They've done a full sweep and there was no one else here.'

One of the SOCO team pushes through the flap of the tent with a number of evidence bags clutched in his gloved hands. John tells him that he is finished with the body for now, and wants it at the lab as soon as possible.

It.

Simon is already an *it*, I think to myself. A thing. An object. From years of experience, I know that it's best to look at a crime scene, and a body, as dispassionately as possible. But, when that body is someone you knew, someone you had been having a laugh with mere hours ago, dispassionate is easier said than done. Believe me, I've tried it before.

John leaves the scene, and the roar of his engine moments later rips through the quiet of the night. The SOCO bends down and takes the rose from Simon's outstretched hand, placing it carefully inside a clear bag, careful not to let the thorns tear the plastic.

Having been so focussed on the rose and the horrific injuries, I'd not noticed what was in the other hand. The SOCO uses a pair of tweezers to pull a single strand of hair from Simon's left hand. He places it directly into another evidence bag, before sealing it and holding it up to the light. The hair is about thirty centimetres long and a dark brown colour.

I silently thank Simon for this break in the case. The hair can hopefully be linked by DNA to someone already on the system. That someone being Johnny.

A short while later, the body is moved. I walk into the hallway of the house. All around me, the forensic team are busily and methodically going about their business, combing every inch of the house, both downstairs and up. Martin greets me with a sombre look and tells me that so far, nothing seems out of the ordinary.

Except for one thing.

I follow him over the stepping plates from the hallway into the living room. The room is sparsely decorated and neatly organised. Highlights from the day's football matches are playing on a widescreen TV and a book case rests against one wall. A polished glass coffee table in the middle of the room houses an assortment of magazines, the covers arranged artfully, partially obscuring each other. On the same coffee table are two flute glasses and an unopened bottle of prosecco with a colourful label.

'You think he was expecting company?' Martin asks, pointing at the corked bottle and the empty glasses.

'He said he was meeting someone, in Zebra earlier…'

'Zebra?' Martin interrupts.

'It's a bar on the main street. Upmarket place. He said he was going on a first date.'

'Maybe he was counting his chickens, assuming he was going to get the lassie to come back home with him.'

I shake my head.

'That's not the way Simon is. Was.'

I walk across to the table and put a gloved hand on the bottle. Still cold.

'I met him at seven o'clock and I got the message at just after midnight. There's no way that, if he'd left the bottle out before leaving to meet me, that it would still be chilled.'

I take a few minutes to have a think. The position of his body, the prosecco and the tidy house all point to one thing.

'Purely speculation at this stage, but here's what I think. For some reason, he didn't meet his date at the bar. Maybe she messaged him to say that she was running late or whatever. Somehow, it was suggested that they meet up later, at his. From what I know about Simon, I assume it was at her suggestion. He came home via an off licence, tidied up and got the drinks ready. When the knock on the door came, he answered expecting her, but was greeted by thin air.'

I think of his shining shoes resting on the exterior doormat.

'I think he stepped outside to see if there was anyone there, and was clubbed in the face from the darkness.'

'So, you think this woman he was supposed to be on a date with did this?

I shrug my shoulders, a theory emerging that needs some development before being shared.

'I take it you haven't found his phone,' I say.

'I think the killer probably pocketed it when he sent you the picture. We'll never see it again, but we might get lucky with cell site analysis.'

He sounds less than convincing. What would more than likely happen is that the killer would take the SIM card out and discard both somewhere far away from the crime scene, meaning we couldn't track the phone. No, Johnny Mayhem is far too calculating and prepared to be caught by such a simple mistake.

'What about the hair?' I ask.

'Hard to tell much just from looking at it. I wanted to get it bagged as quickly as I could, to make sure not a modicum of evidence could escape. It's quite long, which would suggest it isn't one of Simon's. That's where I think your Johnny Mayhem theory falls down. When he left prison, he had short hair. There's no way it could grow to that length in the time he's been out. We'll test it against what we have in the system. Should be able to have the results to you by tomorrow.'

'Nothing else to see?' I ask.

'Nope,' he answers, shaking his head. 'All clear upstairs and nothing in the kitchen. We'll work our magic, see if there are any prints other than his.'

He tells me that he'll keep me in the loop and walks off. Not wanting to annoy the SOCOs by milling around aimlessly, I go outside into the smaller tent and take my protective suit off. As I approach the cordon, the uniformed officer points me in the direction of an elderly gentleman, who is standing in the doorway of his house with a dressing gown pulled tight across his body. He invites me over with a flick of his fingers.

He introduces himself as Derek Surgenor. The moonlight is reflected on his bald head and intelligent eyes peer out from behind thick rimmed glasses. He invites me into his house, telling me that he has something that may be of use.

We walk through a wide hall, my boots thumping on the tiled floor. When we get to the kitchen, he takes a seat in a padded chair and pulls himself up to a desktop computer and turns the monitor on. The screensaver shows a faraway beach, the calm waters drifting over white sands as it greets the shore.

I look away as he keys in a password and when I look back, I can see a grainy image of outside his house.

'CCTV. Barry across the road got a Jaguar last year and we both agreed we'd get cameras to be safe. Thieves have been known to operate in the area. We thought about setting up a neighbourhood watch, but it seemed a lot of work. Anyway, Barry watched my cameras get installed and then told me that that would probably be enough security, and that he needn't bother. Cheap bastard,' he laughs. 'I'm the only one with a camera on the street so I thought you might like to look through it, in the event it may help with whatever is happening outside.'

He gets up from his seat and sets the kettle to boil. When it clicks, he makes two cups of tea and sets one on the table beside me. He retreats wordlessly into the living room with a mug of his own.

Rather than trawl through all the footage now, I double check what time the text message with the picture of Simon's body was received and fast forward the footage to fifteen minutes before that. I imagine that the picture was snapped in the seconds after Simon had been beaten to death and sent as soon as possible after that.

I press play on the footage and immediately my hope that it may be of use goes south. If anything is happening on the screen, it's difficult to make out. The black and white footage is grainy enough to start with. The lashing rain interrupts the video further—the white lines only adding to my annoyance. I put the video on double speed and watch the night pass by without interruption.

Suddenly, there is movement. There are tall, well-kept hedges on both sides of Derek's garden and no car, so the field of vision is excellent, even if the camera used to record it is not. From the right-hand side of the video a figure appears. It walks with purpose past Derek's garden and is gone again. I rewind and watch the short amount of footage a number of times, though trying to ascertain any detail from the two second snippet is impossible. I make a note of the time that the figure enters the video and press play again, letting the footage roll. Not long after, the figure reappears, walking in the opposite direction, back towards the entrance of the cul-de-sac. Again, they do not turn their head and I am only offered an unclear profile shot of whoever killed Simon.

I call for Derek and he shuffles into the room, his slippers gliding across the linoleum. I ask him if it would be okay to send a computer technician in the morning to take a copy of the footage, and he readily agrees. I thank him for his time, take one final sip of the hot tea and prepare to head outside into the cold night.

The crowd at the cordon have dispersed, probably having realised that the scene is so well covered that they weren't going to get a peep of anything. The uniformed officer is still keeping vigil at the tape, though not by choice, judging by the pissed off scowl on his face as the water drips from the peak of his hat onto nose and chin.

As I walk to my car, safe in the knowledge that Simon's house is in capable hands with Martin and the SOCO team, I consider what tomorrow will bring. We have a hair, the rose and some poor-quality video footage of the killer approaching the house and leaving again.

I find myself pinning all my hopes of Ross Powell's considerable technological knowhow. If he can work his magic on the video, we may be able to get a clear look at the person stalking past Derek's house with murder on their mind. We might be able to make out discernible features; hair colour or if they were wearing glasses, or, best case scenario—Johnny Mayhem is revealed in all his glory.

Johnny may have thought he was clever, coming in the dead of night and taking revenge on the man who had arrested him all those years ago. He may have thought he was sticking two fingers up to the police by leaving the rose in Simon's hand; his calling card, his way of bragging to the police that he is smarter than us.

But he hadn't banked on the fact that an old fella wanted to help his mate protect his fancy car from potential thieves. If we can trace his movements, we might be able to track him to his hideout.

My stomach fizzes with the excitement of a breakthrough as I indicate out of the street and make my way home.

AS SOON AS my head touches the pillow, Leo's cries fill the upstairs. I'd closed the door quietly and made my way up the stairs without light or sound in an effort not to disturb him.

No dice, it would seem.

Tom rolls over and tells me that he has been in three times with him. I assume from his tone and the way he immediately rolled over again that despite me having been working most of the night, that it is my turn to soothe Leo. I throw the covers off and traipse in the baby's room.

Thankfully, replacing the dummy into his open mouth seems to do the trick. I watch the darkened outline of his body splay out like a starfish, content in the peace that the dummy has given him.

Questions start to whirl around my mind.

By spending so much time embroiled in the case, am I being a bad mother? The reason I'd moved to a desk job after the last case was so that I could have a rigid structure in my work, to allow time to be a mum. The thing I'd always wanted. Now, I berate myself for putting more emphasis on the job. I realise I was naïve in thinking that the thugs and killers of the city would work around my schedule.

I stroke the soft skin of his cheek one last time and make my way to bed, hopeful that that will be the last interruption I am faced with tonight.

15

I PUT MY head on my desk and curse the day.

After a fitful sleep that seemed all too brief, I find myself back at work, staring at my very full email inbox. I spend the next half an hour sorting through the messages that require my urgent attention, content to leave the rest on the 'laterbase'.

I check my list of things to do today. The first requires a short road trip. I leave my room and walk over to Andy's desk, telling him that I need him to come with me. He finishes the paperwork he was completing and jumps up, pulling his coat on over his stripy shirt.

'Where we off to, boss?' he asks.

'The pub,' I answer.

'THIS ISN'T A PUB,' he says, looking up at the minimalistic façade of Zebra. 'This is one of those fancy pants bars that don't serve a decent lager but do sell organic scrumpy to be a bit *out there*.'

He's right of course, but I don't give him the satisfaction of telling him that. Instead, I stride up to the door and knock. Despite the early hour, lights blossom from inside into the drizzly day outside, so we know that someone is in there. Footsteps sound from within and a few seconds later, a key turns in the lock and the heavy door is pushed open.

Relief spreads over me when I recognise the barman from last night. We introduce ourselves formally and he ushers us inside. He crouches and makes his way through the low opening, reappearing behind the bar.

It seems that, before he was interrupted, the barman was in the process of scrubbing away the previous night. A faint whiff of disinfectant taints the air and a mop bucket rests against one of the booths, the chairs stacked upside down on the tables. A wet rag lies limp on the grubby bar.

'What can I do you for?' he asks, as Andy and I pull ourselves onto a bar stool.

'I was in last night…'

'I remember you,' he interrupts. 'You were sat in the corner with a gentleman over there. I remember you because of the look on your face when I told you the price of a couple of pints.'

'I need to work on my poker face,' I say, allowing myself a laugh.

'So, how can I help you?'

'If you remember me, you must remember the man I was with. I was just wondering, when I left, did he have company?'

The barman shakes his head.

'No, when you left, he sat sipping on the pint you'd bought for him. Phil and I were laughing about what a tight arse he was. When he finished his drink, he came up and asked if we were showing the football. I told him we weren't. We don't have a licence and the clientele here aren't interested in sports, so we didn't bother putting in TVs. He set his empty pint on the bar and left.'

'Did he speak to anyone on the phone whilst he was here?'

'No. He was texting or something on it a lot, but no speaking to anyone.'

'Is there anywhere around here that shows football?' Andy asks.

He suggests that The Anchor might've been where Simon went next. We follow his lead, and thankfully, the manager of The Anchor remembers him, on account of his request to have the Preston North End game on. He recalls that he bought a pint and sat on a bar stool, watching the game. No one came to meet him and at the end of the night, left alone and disappointed, as Preston succumbed to a 4-1 drubbing at the hands of fierce rivals Blackburn Rovers.

We thank him for his time and drive back to the station.

The theory that started to develop in my head is close to becoming a fully-fledged, almost sharable notion.

WHEN I GET back to my office, I have an email from Martin.

The hair that was found at the crime scene has been tested for DNA and, unfortunately, for the case, does not belong to Johnny Mayhem. Nor does it belong to any other human, as it turns out the hair is synthetic. In essence, the hair that was found is a single strand from a wig. The information slots in nicely with my developing theory and as another welcome email pings into my inbox, I call for a briefing.

THE ROOM FILLS quickly. Though Simon was no longer a police officer, he is still thought of as one of us, such is the unity and togetherness of the force. Everyone assembled is keen to see justice done as swiftly as possible.

I take to the front of the room and wheel the case board into view. Tacked to it are a number of pictures, including those of Simon's bloodied and battered face and the rose in his hand.

These are the ones I start with.

'The body of Simon Black was discovered at his house last night. We believe it is the work of Johnny Mayhem, owing to the placement of the lavender rose in his hand. We are obviously linking it with the murder of Duane Miller. The media are going to be crawling all over this, so we need to step it up. We believe he died from blunt force trauma to the head.'

The pictures of his destroyed face back up my claim. Notes are scribbled and I give everyone a minute to soak up the information. Many in the room knew him and many will be keen to make sure that the assailant is captured as soon as possible.

'The murder weapon—a baseball bat—was recovered in some nearby woodland this morning. Martin has had it dusted for prints already. Only one set is evident and they belong to Mayhem. The phone of the deceased is unaccounted for. I was sent a text message from it, by Mayhem, so we believe the phone was taken and destroyed. The SIM can't be tracked.'

More scribbles.

'A dark strand of plastic, believed to have been separated from a wig, was also found at the scene. The synthetic hair is about thirty centimetres long.'

'Didn't I hear that Simon was on a date last night?' someone chirps up from the back. 'Are we discounting the woman?'

Time to let my theory run wild.

'I don't think there ever was a woman. I believe he was being catfished. When I spoke to Simon last night, he told me that he and this mystery woman he met on the internet had only ever contacted each other by message. No phone calls. I think Johnny Mayhem was posing as a single woman. They arranged to meet at a bar, then Simon got a text to say that the woman was running late and might not make it. I'm only guessing here, but judging by the bottle of prosecco and the two glasses in his front room, I think it was suggested that they meet at his house. When he answered the door, instead of a pretty woman greeting him, it was the blunt end of a baseball bat.'

I can sense some sceptics in the room.

'How would Johnny have known that Simon was on a dating site?' asks someone.

I'd been wondering that myself.

'I don't know,' I admit. 'Perhaps he found out, somehow, that Simon was a middle-aged, single man and took a chance.'

Murmurs of disbelief fill the room and I know that the explanation sounds flimsy, but at this stage, it's all I can offer. Ross Powell is currently trying to work his magic on the dating site angle, but with nothing concrete, I can't offer much more.

'What about with Duane?' a thick set officer in the middle row asks.

'Elaborate,' I say.

'Well, let's say that Mayhem did don a wig and stilettos and wobble his way up to Simon's front door before battering him to death. He couldn't have done that with Duane. Duane knew what he looked like.'

'Duane and him were mates, though,' I answer. 'It's a completely different situation. I doubt he'd have to have put a miniskirt on to get into Duane's bedroom.'

There is laughter in the room.

'I imagine Duane and Johnny spent many plutonic hours in that bedroom, snorting and smoking all sorts. Sex didn't get Johnny into Duane's bedroom, money did.'

'So, what next?' Andy asks in an attempt to get back to some form of professionalism.

'Next, we find Johnny. The murders occurred only a couple of miles from each other, so we concentrate on that area. He has to be hiding somewhere. DCI Killick is putting a list together of possible targets and assigning protection.'

I end the briefing and walk back into my office, frustrated at the lack of a plan. Johnny is three steps ahead of us and we can't seem to catch up. It seems like we have to wait for him to leave us more clues, more bodies, in the hope that he somehow slips up.

This clearly isn't an option.

Two people have died already. Two too many.

My computer pings. I wiggle the mouse and the screen springs into life. I check my emails to find a message from Ross Powell. He's struggling with the dating sites, as he doesn't know which one was being used. Even if he did, the level of encryption is too high and the privacy of users too protected that he thinks it is a dead end.

The second part of the message is only slightly more optimistic. He has managed to clean up the video, though it's only made a marginal difference. I click on the link and the footage begins.

He has trimmed it to keep the file size small. It begins a few seconds before Johnny emerges from one side of the frame. The face is obscured. No feature is recognisable. The dark mane of hair, which we know is a wig, is shoulder length. The figure is wearing a long, dark coat and the baseball bat can be seen gripped in their left hand, swinging with the motion of the arm.

I rewind the footage time and time again, trying to pick out any detail that might help us. Aside from the obvious, I'm struck by the femininity of the figure's stride.

I pull up a YouTube video of The Darling Roses in their Britpop pomp, watching as Johnny sashays across the stage, hips swinging and arms raised, his facial expressions suggesting he is at one with the music being played by his bandmates. His movements are delicate and definitely are in keeping with that of the shrouded figure from the CCTV.

I'm about to turn the music off when I see a related video that sparks my interest. Glenn Lumb's bearded face fills the thumbnail.

I click on the link and it starts. The guitarist is walking down the street, being pursued by a fan with a camera phone. The footage is shaky and I get the feeling Glenn just wants to be left alone. The fan fires question after question at Glenn's back, but receives no answer. Eventually, he asks a question that must've touched a raw nerve. Glenn turns back and stares at whoever is behind the camera, eyes wild.

'You want to know the truth,' he shouts. 'The truth is no; we will never get back together. I know things about that prick that will stay with me 'til the day I die. I'd rather cut my cock off than share a stage with Johnny again.'

The footage fades to a black screen. Comments underneath the video cast questions about what he was talking about. Some replies suggest things they have read elsewhere, but none seem severe enough to warrant such a vitriolic reaction from Lumb.

I pull my phone out and dial his number, though I know it's a longshot that he'll answer when on tour. Unsurprisingly, it rings out and connects me to his voicemail. I leave a message but am pretty sure that I won't be hearing from him.

The sooner he gets back, the better. It seems a chat with the guitarist has become a necessity.

16

ANDY AND I are shooting the shit in my office, throwing theories at each other about the case. For the last twenty minutes, he's tried, successfully, to pick holes in my 'Mayhem as a woman' theory. The sticking point is the dating site and how someone posing as a woman could just happen upon the person they want to murder.

It's too fucking convenient.

So far, I've not been able to satisfy Andy's questions and, truth be told, I'm losing faith in my own theory. Something just doesn't add up. As we bat ideas back and forward like two blindfolded tennis players, the door to my office bursts open and DCI Killick enters.

'I need both of you in the briefing room, now,' she says, before backing out of the doorway at speed and summoning whoever else she needs on her way.

My pulse quickens. She's usually unflappable, so something must've happened to get her knickers in a twist. Something big.

I follow Andy out of the office and across the open planned office space into the briefing room. The smell of cheap coffee greets us as we find a couple of seats beside each other at the back of the room. The anticipation in the room is palpable. Jennifer Killick is at the front of the room, pacing to and fro, waiting for any stragglers before she starts the meeting.

After a few minutes, when she is sure that everyone she needs is present, she begins.

'We think there has been a sighting of Johnny Mayhem.'

Her words are a defibrillator shot to the chest of a staff being sapped of their morale. The case so far has been a slog. Lots of hours of manpower have been poured into it, for barely an ounce of reward. Everyone in the room sits up straight, eager for every bit of detail they can get.

'A man called the dedicated phoneline, describing someone who he believes to be our perpetrator. The details he gave matched with what we know about Johnny—height, appearance and clothing.'

'Where is he?' Andy asks, unable to take the suspense anymore.

'The caller has watched him come and go from an abandoned mill in the east of the city, not far from his home address. He's seen him a couple of times, leaving and coming back with a bag from the corner shop. I've got a car over there now, keeping watch.'

'How are we playing it?' I ask.

'The tech team are going to do a bit of research on the mill for us. How many doors, places he could potentially run from and what have you. We're going to raid it tonight, under the cover of darkness. You're my team, so what I need you to do is go home, get rested and come back here at midnight. We'll go through what we know about the building, divide into teams and make a plan. Until then, the car stationed outside the mill will keep track of any movement. If he leaves, looking like he's got somewhere to be, I'll call you and we'll get going sooner. Midnight, please,' she says, by way of a dismissal.

I MANAGE TO get some sleep while Leo is at the babysitter's and Tom is at work. It's restless though. I can't stop my subconscious from going through every little detail of tonight, before I even know the plan. My dreams keep bringing up images of police swarming the building and Johnny Mayhem being enveloped in a dark horde of bodies; the defeat etched on a face illuminated by blue flashing lights.

I awake at the sound of the door opening downstairs. Pulling myself from my slumber, I descend the stairs and greet Tom and Leo with hugs. Tom enquires why I am home so early and when I tell him, it's greeted with attempted indifference, though I can see the veins in his neck and forehead flare. A night raid on an abandoned mill in order to catch a suspected murderer is not what constitutes safe, in his eyes.

The rest of the evening passes slowly. I put Leo to bed, reading him a story before letting him snuggle into me. When he has drifted off to the land of nod, I set him carefully in the cot and walk downstairs. Tom and I make an attempt at normality by putting the TV on and enquiring about each other's day. By nine o'clock, I know I am unbearable. My jittering leg drums a rhythm on the sofa that Tom ignores, though I can tell it is annoying him. He heads to bed at eleven, making me promise him that I will be as safe as I can. As he ascends the stairs, I make my way out the door, closing it carefully behind me, and jump into the car.

A BIRD'S EYE view of the mill Mayhem is alleged to be hiding in is on the projector screen. The dirty, grey roof of the dilapidated mill is a rectangular shape, with a smaller square at the front acting as an entrance. A huge chimney climbs skywards, the red brick exterior scrambling towards a vast hole at the top.

Red arrows, superimposed onto the picture, show the doorways dotted around the building. In all, there are ten possible escape routes. One at the front of the building, two at the rear and the rest along either side.

The building is surrounded on three sides by a dense woodland and the front of the mill faces a busy road. This cannot be used for obvious reasons. Johnny might just notice a load of police vehicles driving slowly towards him. It's decided that we park our fleet of vehicles nearby and approach from the rear, using the trees as cover.

Teams are decided and a plan is formulated. To the armed police in the room, this is their bread and butter. They are calm and calculated as discussions about which team will enter through which door unfold. Instructions are given slowly and methodically and, once the plan has been finalised and ran through a couple of times, it's go time.

THE JOURNEY TO the rendezvous point isn't a long one, though it feels like it is taking an age. I sit in the back of the van, scenarios whirling through my mind.

What ifs after what ifs.

My bit in the evening is minor compared to the armed police flanking me. They are the one putting their bodies on the line, while I wait for the carnage to die down and do the detective work after.

My leg is jittering again; the solitary bit of movement in the back of the van, save for a few jaws chewing gum. There's almost a feeling of tranquillity. Everyone knows their job and each person knows that they are good at it. The plan of attack is secure in their heads and will be executed as such.

After what feels like an aeon, we pull up in a layby on a road to the rear of the mill. The elevation means, if the trees weren't surrounding the expanse of bricks, we'd be looking down on its roof.

We split into the teams and climb over the metal barrier that separates the main road from the copse of tall oaks. Slowly and noiselessly, we make our way down the steep bank, using the trunks as cover, making sure we can't be seen on the off-chance Johnny is waiting by a window. I check my watch and the illuminated face tells me that it's just approaching three o'clock in the morning.

The thick clouds in the sky prevent any moonlight from reaching us, and, coupled with the dense tree canopy and remote location, it's hard to see where I am going. Branches scratch at my face and more than once I trip over adventuring roots, causing me to curse under my breath. Luckily, everyone is in the same boat.

We eventually reach the tree line and have our first unobstructed view of the mill. The bricks seem black in real life, as if centuries worth of grime and toil are stored within them.

Large window frames pepper the building, though I can't find one pane of glass still intact. The chimney towers ominously above us, keeping a watchful eye on us, reminding us just how insignificant human life can seem.

The crackle of static sounds as communication devices are tested one last time. Thumbs ups are flashed in every direction. Deep breaths and murmurs of good luck are passed around. Focus descends and on the count of three, the teams scurry in all directions towards their intended destinations. One member of each team carries an Enforcer—a metal battering ram half a metre long, capable of applying three tonnes of pressure; enough to make short work of most doors. The other two team members carry guns.

We make it to our doorway. Andy and I stand back from the action. In front of us are the two armed police officers and in front of them is the man with the ram. Whilst we wait for the signal, time seems to slow. The wind flicks lazily at the leaves on the trees, as if nature itself is aware what a big moment this is in the case. The man at the front of our group zeroes in on a spot on the door, just below the rusted handle and lock. He swings the battering ram in the air, as if gauging its weight for the first time despite being well more than well acquainted.

A noise in my ear makes me jump. The final team confirm they are in place and ready to go. The bristle of anticipation touches even the hardest of hearts. Mantras are whispered and final prayers are uttered. Someone starts a countdown that is being relayed to every single person here.

Five.

An eternity seems to pass before the next number, though in reality it is a single second.

Four.

Sweat causes the shirt I'm wearing to stick to my armpits.

Three.

Two.

One.

A collective intake of breath.

'Go, go, go!'

The splintering of doors echo around the mill as every team's leading man lands a knockout blow with the battering ram.

Each lead steps out of the way as armed police swarm the building with guns raised. Discordant yelling, designed to confuse and disorientate the target swirls around the building. It certainly does a number on me, and I'm stood safely outside. I can't comprehend what must be going through Johnny's head.

After a few minutes, the noise dissipates and quiet reigns.

'Secure,' someone says over the radio.

Andy and I step in through the doorway, over the ruined door and into the centre of the cavernous room. Disused machinery takes up most of the floorspace, long abandoned from its original purpose. Rats scurry in the shadows and drug paraphernalia litters the concrete floor.

'In the corner,' one of the armed police tells me, pointing to where he means.

Andy and I make our way over at pace.

A man in a green parka is on his knees, facing away from us, with his hands cupped on the back of his head, fingers interlaced. A discarded kitchen knife lies near the sleeping bag he had probably been encased in only a few minutes ago. His breathing is erratic, most likely on account of the adrenaline flowing through his veins.

'Keep your hands where we can see them and turn around. Slowly,' I say.

He does.

17

JOHNNY'S EYES PART slowly, a thick fog obscuring his thoughts. Blinking, he looks around the cramped, dank space and remembers where he is.

He pushes the thin sheet off his body and stands up. He can't reach his full height as the ceiling is much too low, but he stretches as much as the space will allow him. His knees crack and a muscle pops in his neck, spraying pain down his back. Cursing, he rubs at the nape of his neck with a grubby hand and sits down on his thin mattress.

He lifts the newspaper that has been delivered and shakes his head at the headline. At the incompetence of the police.

Apparently, they'd mounted a full-on raid of a mill, in the hope of catching him last night. The junkie who they'd scared the life out of had run straight to the media and told his story.

Greater Manchester Police had issued an apology this morning, relaying to the press that they were following a reliable tip-off in the hope of apprehending a killer.

Of course, they hadn't mentioned his name. But it was implied.

There could only be one dangerous killer rock star that they were searching for.

A hollow laugh that hurt his throat escaped his lips as he looked around where he was staying. He wished he had the luxury of a fucking mill to roam about in. Instead, he had a low ceilinged, freezing area not much bigger than his utility room at home.

Still, at least he had a mattress.

Sleep was the great restorer.

He fell back onto his pillow and read the paper cover to cover, taking in everything he could about the failed raid.

It was interesting to know that they were piling so many resources into finding him. He laughed again. He had a feeling that they could look for the rest of their lives and they'd never come close to finding him.

Not until it was too late, anyway.
Now, on to other matters.
What was we he going to do next?

18

I WIPE THE remainder of Leo's breakfast from his chin and release him from his high chair. We go into the living room and get some of his toys out, before lying on the carpet and playing together. I marvel at how his little fingers reach for the toy car and proceed to push it up a ramp on the plastic car park Tom had found in a charity shop.

My thoughts drift. I'm in the ramshackle mill, watching the man swivel on the spot with a multitude of guns trained on him. The terrified look on his face is one I won't forget in a while. In the end, it hadn't been Johnny Mayhem at all, just an unfortunate soul that happened to dress similarly. The news had broken the story early this morning, with the man himself being interviewed. He'd exaggerated some of the details somewhat, but the crux of the story was true. The DCI has a meeting booked in with the head honcho later today to explain the failed mission and the apparent waste of resources, and I do not envy her one bit.

My attention is drawn away from my thoughts by the recognisable voice on the television. I turn and find I'm staring into the eyes of Michael Sims; the presenter of the Johnny Mayhem documentary. He looks like he hasn't much sleep in the past week; dark bags have gathered underneath his eyes and a scraggy beard has formed.

The female presenter of the morning show, who looks far too awake for this time of the morning, introduces him whilst he gives a smarmy wave to the camera.

'So, can you tell the viewers why you are here today?' she says.

'I've come on today to tell you, the country and the world that there is a story going out on the news this evening at 6pm

GMT that you will not want to miss. It really is going to—what is it the kids say these days? *Break the internet.*'

'And, can you give us a clue as to what the story is about?' she asks, glancing off screen.

'I can't tell you the information that the article will contain. But, I can tell you what subject it will concern.'

He pauses in order to ham up the drama and looks straight down the camera lens.

'It turns out Amanda Mayhem had a few secrets that I've managed to uncover.'

The female presenter spends the next few minutes trying to extract more information from him, but Michael is a closed trap. He simply repeats that the story will break later today, and that the public will not want to miss it. When the program cuts to the slightly eccentric weatherman, I grab the remote and turn to CBeebies. The jaunty theme tune to Peppa Pig tears Leo away from his game. His eyes light up as Daddy Pig snorts and the program begins.

I pull my phone from my pocket and phone the station. Angela answers after a few rings.

'Get in touch with Michael Sims as soon as you can, and transfer him to me.'

She tells me that she will crack on with the task straight away and will be in contact as soon as she gets him. I hang up and set the phone down on the table.

I don't know what information Michael Sims has, or whether it is even legit. But, one thing is for certain, it's best for everyone, including his own safety, that whatever private information he is sending out to the world remains unseen. Johnny Mayhem requires no more ammunition.

I only hope we can get that message to him before tonight.

WITH LEO ASLEEP in his cot, I phone Andy.

'You heard anything?' I ask, once the pleasantries are done with.

'Yes. We heard back from Johnny's bank. They've told us that the last transaction on any of his cards was on the night he had the shoving match with Duane in Havana. He bought some drinks in the club and also took £250 from a cash machine on the same road.'

'And it's not been used since?'

'Nope,' he confirms.

'So, he's been living off 250 quid this whole time?'

'Well,' Andy says. 'I've been thinking about that. It seems unlikely that a man of his expensive taste could survive on so little. We know he was after heroin, so chances are he's gone elsewhere to get that. Which means that he probably has money stashed somewhere else. Which leads me to point two. We haven't been able to find any properties linked to him that we don't already know about.'

'Have those been searched?'

'The flats in Chelsea and Edinburgh have, yes. No sign of him. We're waiting to hear back from the police in Ibiza. But we've checked with border patrol and Johnny's passport hasn't been used, so it's almost impossible that he would've made it to Spain.'

'Thanks, Andy. I'll be in later today—I'm having a bit of time with the little one. Would you mind sending uniforms out to talk to known drug dealers again? If Johnny is using again, someone must've dealt to him. I know we've tried once, and that it's unlikely anyone will tell us anything; they'll all claim they've stopped dealing, but it's worth a shot.'

'No problem,' he says, before hanging up.

I sink into the sofa and close my eyes. Michael Sims face fills the blackness—the smug look plastered over it because he knows he has got the world waiting with bated breath. I think of Amanda Mayhem's body, and hope that whatever he has found might help us with the case.

I open the Twitter app on my phone to find the newsfeed flooded with theories about what information Michael is sitting on, as well as hashtags like #WhatDidAmandaDo, dedicated to unfounded speculation. No good will come of wading through what the minds of internet trolls have to offer, so I throw the phone to the other end of the sofa.

In the time since my phone call to Angela this morning, I've reconsidered. Michael Sims's information might be just the thing we need. It might force Johnny out from wherever he is hiding. Killers make mistakes when they are rash. And stoking up the ashes that lie within Johnny might just be the way to trip him up. Butterflies flutter in my stomach as I check my watch. Only a few more hours until the story breaks…

SUSIE, LILY AND JILL are already poring over menus when I arrive.

'Sorry I'm late,' I say, pushing hair out of my eyes as I take the vacant seat at the table. One of the babies is asleep in its pushchair and the other is sitting in a high chair, happily sucking on a colourful dummy. They tell me not to worry about my tardiness and pass me a menu once Leo is strapped securely into the highchair beside me. As I look down the list of food, I suddenly realise how hungry I am.

The waitress approaches our table and takes our orders. Lily, Jill and I order food, though Susie opts for a large black coffee.

'I went out last night,' she says, almost apologetically. 'Adam was at his dad's and a few friends were going out, so I thought why not!?'

'Are you feeling rough today?' I ask.

She nods. 'I haven't had a drop of alcohol since before I got pregnant so it didn't take much and I may have overindulged. My head is banging and I've got to pick Adam up later. I'm hoping the coffee helps.'

We descend into gossip about her night in the city, living vicariously through her. She tells us how, even though she is not romantically linked with the baby's father, she still felt resistant to accepting drinks from willing men. Shortly after, our food arrives and the conversation dies. Susie blows on her coffee and takes a few sips. Her phone beeps in her bag and she reaches in to get it. She lets out a frustrated whine and her fingers race over the screen, before she throws the phone into her bag again.

'Matt wants me to pick up Adam early,' she says, standing up and taking her jacket from the back of the chair. 'Apparently, he has somewhere more important to be.'

We say our goodbyes as she exits the café and marches past the window and out of sight towards the car park. Conversation turns to Susie's unusual situation—young baby, seemingly nice father who she doesn't want to be romantically involved with but does want involved in the baby's life. After that, we cover lack of sleep, being back at work and missing sex drives before paying for the bill and leaving. I check the time and realise that I only have twenty minutes to get home, before Michael's exclusive breaks.

TOM AND I sit on the sofa, Leo bouncing on my knee, as the jingle for the news plays. When the music ends, the screen shows Katie Lewis, the well-known newsreader, sitting behind the desk staring po-faced at the camera. After a solemn greeting, she introduces the first story. A picture of Amanda Mayhem marching vivaciously down a catwalk dressed in a ridiculous outfit appears above her left shoulder.

'Photographs of Amanda Mayhem and an unknown male have surfaced, leading to speculation that she was having an affair before her untimely murder. The photographs show the model, who is wearing large sunglasses and a baseball cap, presumably to try and hide her appearance, cosying up to a handsome man in a secluded area of a park. Another shows the two kissing in a parked car. We have the man responsible for breaking the story here with us tonight, Mr Michael Sims.'

Michael is trying his best to match Katie's grave expression, but failing spectacularly. He is wearing a different suit to earlier and looks a tad more rested. Although, perhaps the BBC news have a better make-up team than the ITV breakfast program do.

'Mr Sims,' she says, 'can you give us a bit more background on the photographs?'

'I can,' he smiles. 'The one of them hugging on the bench was taken in a park in Marple, a suburb of Manchester, my source tells me. The other, in the parked car, is harder to place.'

'And how did you come across these photographs?'

He taps his nose at the question. 'I'm afraid my source would prefer to remain anonymous. You can understand the hate they'd receive, especially in such vitriolic times.'

'So why release the photos at all?' Katie says, annoyance creeping into her voice.

'I thought, with the hunt for Johnny Mayhem ongoing, it would be beneficial for the public to know a bit more about the case.'

'You mean,' she says, 'you saw the opportunity for a bit of publicity and leapt at the chance. Don't you think that releasing these is unethical? What about the man in the pictures? Isn't he entitled to privacy?'

A lesser man would be intimated by the aggravation in her voice. But not Michael. He seems to be enjoying it.

'Look, if you're going to have an affair, very publicly might I add, then why would you be surprised if it appears in the media? She was very well known by this point and they clearly weren't concerned with privacy then, so why should we be now?'

As they continue to talk, the photographs being discussed appear side-by-side on the screen. Whoever took them had been standing quite a distance away, presumably using their camera phone. The quality isn't great, but even at range Amanda's perfect features are clear to see. The same cannot be said of the man. His long, dark hair is obscuring his face in both photos. I doubt even Ross Powell could enhance them enough to make a positive ID. The photos disappear from view and the segment ends. The camera moves back to focus solely on Katie, who doesn't look quite as composed now.

I turn the TV off and think about Michael's reasons for releasing them. Publicity is undoubtably what he had in mind when he decided to cash in the photos. People up and down the country will be talking about them for weeks to come, and in doing so, talking about him. He probably saw this as his way of escaping the C-list.

I mull over other possible explanations and can't think of any. It's irresponsible journalism at best. At worst, Michael's story may just have poured petrol onto Johnny Mayhem's fire. I only hope that the man's identity remains a secret.

19

"SO, SHE WAS having an affair," Johnny thinks to himself. At the time, he'd suspected something, though had dismissed it as there had never been any evidence. Turns out, she had just been very careful.

He reads the newspaper cover to cover and when he's done, lies back on his bed, if you could call it that, and stares into the eyes of the man who had fucked his wife. His eyes scan the page and lock onto the name of the man who broke the story, the man he himself had spilled his guts to on camera. Well, this certainly changes things—he now knows who the next two victims will be.

20

THE ATMOSPHERE IN the briefing room is tense. Everyone is talking in raised voices about the exclusive from last night concerning Amanda Mayhem's affair and blasting Michael Sims for such short-sightedness in releasing the story at this time.

In the end, Ross Powell was not needed to work his magic on the grainy pictures procured by Sims. The tabloid press had done what they do best, and within twelve hours had identified the man cosying up to the model in those photos. By this morning, his face was plastered across the front page of all of the newspapers. Even the reputable ones.

As I'd walked into the petrol station to pay for my full tank of fuel, crystal clear blue eyes had stared back at me from newspaper rack. Eyes that I had recognised at once. They belonged to Eli, the man who had spilled beer over my top at Glenn's gig the other night.

I'd grabbed as many papers as I could carry and taken them to the till. The server had looked at me like I was crazy, and I offered no explanation. I paid her and left as quickly as I could, racing to the station. I pass the newspapers along the rows of officers and get the attention of everyone in the room.

'Sorry for the slightly frantic start to the day, but this is time sensitive.' I spilt the room in half. To the people to the left of me, I say, 'The man in the pictures, Eli Parker, is a person of interest in the case. We believe that he may be in danger, and are keen to locate him. This is priority number one. If anyone gets a whiff of an address or a phone number—I need it straight away.'

I dismiss them to begin their job, underlining again how essential it is that we locate him quickly. I now address the people left in the room.

'Obviously, Johnny Mayhem is still at large and untraceable, it would seem. This might lure him out in the open. If he is on some sort of hunt, it would make sense that he comes after Eli. Once we get an address, I need you in that area. It could be that extra feet on the street leads to his capture.'

I dismiss them too and leave the room at the same time. I enter my office and as I turn the computer on, Andy bursts into my room.

'Someone's got a number,' he says, 'they're firing it your way now.'

An email appears on my screen almost instantly containing a number. I thank Andy and tell him to direct the officers as soon as an address comes in. He leaves the room and I pick up the phone, dialling the number from the screen.

A worried voice answers almost immediately. Female.

'Eli? Eli, is that you?'

'My name is Detective Inspector Erika Piper,' I tell her.

'Is Eli with you?' she shouts, hope rearing its head in her voice.

'No, we don't have Eli here. Do you know where he is?'

'No. We had a fight last night once I saw those photos. He never told me about that and I lost my temper. We fought and I told him to get out of the house. I haven't heard from him since. He's not answering his phone and I've called all his friends that I know the numbers for, but they've not heard from him either.'

I tell her not to worry, that he is probably safe somewhere and using the time to cool down and get his head around the revelation. She tells me her name; Jane, their address and her mobile number. We agree to keep in touch—to inform each other as soon as Eli makes contact. She also gives us his mobile number in case we can find his location that way.

When the call is finished, I walk out of my office and shout the address that Jane has just given us. The team tasked with getting to that area are already heading towards the door as I finish. I go back to my desk and key in Eli's mobile number, but it goes straight to voicemail.

I phone Ross and pass Eli's number his way, putting him in charge of securing a location if possible. I hang up and turn back to the computer. I type his name in to google. Amongst the most recent articles detailing his affair with Amanda are links to his social media pages. I click on the twitter link and spend a few minutes scrolling through his posts. It seems he mainly uses the platform to discuss films and books. There are seventeen photos, though none of him or his wife.

I lock the screen and walk into the open office, locating Angela at her computer.

'No word back from Michael?' I ask.

She shakes her head.

'No, his receptionist or PA or whatever said he was in meetings all day today.'

'Do you have the address of his offices?'

'Yes,' she says, her fingers whizzing over the keys of her computer. On her screen, an image of a fancy glass building appears, the address in a box underneath accompanied by a map.

She prints the details for me and I march over to Andy, who is immersed in an article concerning Eli and Amanda. I read along over his shoulder, though it is just the same known details rehashed.

'We're overnighting,' I tell him. 'Meet me at Stockport train station in an hour.'

21

THE 11.23 FROM Stockport to London Euston is packed to the rafters with football fans. Despite the yard arm not yet having reached midday, lads in red swig from beer cans and boorish behaviour abounds. Chants about various London football teams, sung discordantly, fill the carriage. They shout out over one another, eager to be the one to start the next chant. Over the next half an hour, Liverpool and Manchester City are targeted with songs ranging from funny to vile. After which, worn vocal cords are tended to with more beer.

'Best not let them hear my Scouse accent,' Andy whispers. 'We won't get a moment's peace otherwise.'

We spend the time trying to ignore the hubbub while poring over the case notes, keen to find any small detail that will blow the case open and help us find where Johnny is hiding out. I check my phone, hopeful that Eli Parker will have been found, but there has been no communication from anyone at the station.

I study the folder of words until they become a black blur. Instead, I close my eyes and try to remember any pertinent details from the two crime scenes so far.

The meaning of the roses is obvious. A simple calling card.

The pocket watch stopped at seven o'clock and stuffed into Duane's jacket is slightly odder. Was it simply a message from Johnny to Duane that the bullet to the back of the head was payback for the drug dealer having left it seven years to 'discover' the evidence that freed the rockstar from jail? If so, was Duane even shown the watch before he died, or was it placed there after he'd been killed as an extra clue for the police in case the rose hadn't been enough?

And then there is the distorted CCTV footage of Johnny advancing towards Simon's house. This time, the rose was deemed to have sufficed as a clue. Unless Johnny planted the synthetic hairs in Simon's other hand as the life had ebbed out of him.

If so, why?

Is he trying to show the police that he is a number of steps ahead of us at all times and can afford to play with us by leaving a trail of breadcrumbs?

Or, does he *want* to be caught?

The riotous fans get off at Milton Keynes, pouring out of the train in a red wave that surges into the one and only pub in the train station. There is a collective relaxed exhalation in the carriage, thankful for some quiet for the rest of the journey. I stash my notes back into my bag and think ahead to our meeting with Michael today while Andy snores, his head tilted back with a thin trickle of drool running down his chin.

The endless countryside soon turns to grey and the buildings become taller as we journey towards the centre of the capital. Just before we reach Euston, Andy jerks awake, confusion and sleep mingling as he attempts to remember where he is. He rubs the tiredness away from his eyes and flashes me a weary smile, apologising if he was snoring.

A disembodied voice informs us that we are approaching the end of the line and reminding all passengers to have their tickets ready for inspection. We check that we have lifted all of our belongings before shuffling out of our seats and joining the queue in the gangway. As the train jolts to a stop, the case belonging to the person in front of me collides painfully with my shin bone. Injury turns to insult as the owner turns around to pick up the case, makes eye contact with me before turning round without an apology. I hold my tongue, but behind me I can hear Andy mutter something about rude Southerners.

We disembark and walk to the gates, passing our tickets through the barrier which permits us access to London. Following instructions on Andy's phone, we walk to a nearby tube station and descend the steps into the haze of the underground. Having never really been to London, the regularity of tube trains astounds me. There seems to be one scheduled for every minute of the day. One screeches to a halt beside us and we take a short journey on the Metropolitan line to Farringdon.

Upon climbing to street level again, Andy pulls out his phone and types the address of Michael's office building into the maps app. We follow the blue line on the screen past pubs with colourful baskets of flowers hanging either side of their door and budget hotel chains. The streets are narrower and we receive a few tuts from suited Londoners who regard the speed we are walking at with vexation.

After ten minutes, we arrive at the place we need.

When I pictured going to London to interview a celebrity— a minor one, granted, but a celebrity all the same—I imagined a spacious room in the sky, the glass walls offering a sweeping panoramic view of the city below, the Thames winding through the streets like a docile snake.

The reality is so disappointing in comparison.

In front of us is a small, red-brick building. A blink and you'd miss it type affair. Certainly not the vast, glass-fronted space Google showed us earlier. The black door is in need of a lick of paint and one of the panes of glass needs replacing, a thin crack running the length of it. Beside the door, a silver plaque tells us that we are in the right place. MS Productions is housed here, along with three other, unrelated businesses.

I press the button next to the production company. A woman greets us in a clipped voice, enquiring who we are. When I tell her, she sounds annoyed.

'I already confirmed on the phone that, unfortunately, Mr Sims is unavailable, as he has meetings booked for the rest of the week. I suggested to your superior that if you wanted to speak to Mr Sims, you should book an appointment. Good day.'

Andy raises his eyebrows at me and I laugh. I press the button next to the graphic design company and a much friendlier voice rings through the intercom, along with the buzz of the door's lock being released. Apparently, Whizz Bizz

Designs aren't quite as selective about who they let in the building, which is good for us. We push through the door and climb the stairs, entering Michael's office.

A tiny waiting room awaits us, the rude receptionist squeezed into a corner behind a flimsy wooden desk with an old desktop monitor resting on it. Before she has time to say a word, I take the four steps required to cross the waiting area and open the door to Michael's office space.

I'm expecting to interrupt a meeting in session, Ari Gold style, but all I'm greeted with is the presenter, alone, sitting behind his only slightly more impressive desk, clutching a bottle of Bushmills whisky. His suit jacket is draped over the back of his chair. His top button is undone and the knot of his tie has been pulled at, causing it to tighten and shrivel. Andy follows me in, followed by the tall receptionist, who is admonishing us for our rudeness at the same time as apologising to Michael for not stopping us in time. I remove my ID card from my pocket and flash it at him.

The presenter waves a tired hand, silencing his helper.

'It's fine,' he says. 'Close the door behind you, and have a word with Ziggy across the landing, tell him to stop letting anyone barge in here.'

She leaves and Michael signals to two plush, velvet seats in front of his desk. We accept his offer and sink into the chairs. We introduce ourselves as he tips the bottle to his lips, wincing as the firewater burns the inside of his mouth, causing his lips to part ever so slightly, allowing a few drops of the nectar coloured liquid to run down his chin.

'I thought I'd be hearing from you sooner rather than later,' he says, replacing the top on the bottle and pushing it to the side of the desk.

'If you'd answered our phone calls, you could've saved us a train ride,' Andy answers. 'This way, it looks like you have got something to hide.'

'I've got nothing to hide,' he spits. 'Ask me anything.'

'You may have just condemned a man to death with your little stunt,' I reply. 'If I were you, I'd lose some of the attitude.'

He runs his hands through already greasy hair and fixes us with a belligerent stare. I pull out a notebook and make a show of setting it on the desk in front of me. I scribble the date at the top, taking my time to make him sweat a little longer.

'First of all, why did you do it? Why put those photos out when you know that Johnny Mayhem is currently wanted for questioning?'

'Why did I do it?' he repeats, as if I've asked him the stupidest question I could think of. 'I did it for the reason anyone in this business does anything. Money.'

'What about the morals? The safety and privacy of another human being?'

He barks out a laugh.

'You hand your soul to the devil when you enter this game. I weighed it up for all of two seconds. Yeah, I might have ruined some lad's marriage, but if you are going to have a very public affair with a very well-known and recognisable celebrity, you've signed away any bit of privacy you were entitled to. I'm just surprised they weren't caught at the time.'

On the train down here, I'd anticipated meeting with someone who perhaps hadn't quite known how big this story would become. Someone who had considered the feelings of the subjects within the pictures.

How foolish I was.

'So, you don't feel bad at all?'

'Why should I? Look around you. I'm in a shit office, if you could even call it that, doing a whole lot of work and earning a shit wage for it. Johnny's three-part documentary was supposed to make me a lot of money, and, more importantly, move me up the ladder. Instead, I'm vilified at the station for not delivering what I'd promised, thanks to Mayhem's no show, and I also don't get my full pay. So, no, I don't feel bad about the decision I made.'

'What about if the male in the pictures gets hurt because of what you've done?'

In reply, he simply shrugs his shoulders before reaching for the drink again. His hand freezes under the weight of my stare and he pulls it back, without the bottle.

'Did Johnny get in touch to explain why he didn't show up for the filming of the third documentary?'

No,' he says, shaking his head. 'I've not heard hide nor hair of him since we filmed the second, in that room where he killed his wife.'

'The judge said he didn't,' Andy interrupts.

'The judge made that decision on flimsy evidence as far as I'm concerned. Even Johnny and his lawyers were surprised at the outcome. They'd already started planning their appeal, though of course Johnny had always maintained his innocence,' he says, with a mirthless laugh. 'Having spent some time in his company, I'd bet my house on it being him.'

'Why?'

'Just the way he is. Intense, secretive, up his own arse. He's told himself the same lie for so many years now, even he believes his own innocence. His mask slipped a couple of times during filming, barking orders at the camera crew and storming out of the room when someone brought tea instead of coffee. He's a hothead who thinks he is smarter than he is. But the past will catch up with him.'

He gets up and walks to the window, which overlooks a small park. He rests his head on the glass and breaths deeply, before turning back to us and retaking his place in his seat. On the window pane, a smudge of grease has been left behind, distorting the green of the tree's leaves that are blowing in the wind.

'How did you come to be in possession of the photos?' I ask.

'Someone sent them here. No note, no name, just the photos.'

'Do you still have the envelope?'

He shakes his head.

'Sorry, I binned it. Didn't think it would become a police matter, if I'm honest.'

'Do you still have the photos?'

This time he nods.

'They are in the safe at my house. I imagine them fetching a pretty penny in the not so distant future,' he says, rubbing his hands together like a James Bond villain.

His face falls and his hands separate when I inform him that I'm going to need those photos to test them for fingerprints. He pleads with me to leave them as they are, imploring me not to ruin them with the dust the SOCOs use.

With nothing else to learn and a promise to send the photos to us as a matter of urgency, we get out of our seats and turn to leave.

'Look,' he says. 'I wasn't being entirely truthful earlier. If something bad were to happen to the guy in the photos…'

'Eli Parker,' I interrupt.

'If something were to happen to him, I would feel bad. I'm not a monster. Please, if there is anything I can do to help, let me know.'

He hands me a business card with the logo of his company on it, complete with email address and two phone numbers. I slip it into my pocket and turn towards the door, leaving him to wallow in his own misery.

It seems money and fame aren't all they're cracked up to be.

22

I SET MY bottle of beer down on the ledge with a thud and get my game face on. Andy pushes a small, white ball through a hole and immediately begins rotating handles on the side of the table. His blue team nudge the ball towards my goalmouth before his striker finishes clinically, slotting the ball past my immobile keeper. Andy holds one hand in the air and mimics running off, a la Alan Shearer in his goalscoring pomp.

'I wasn't even ready!' I whine, picking the ball out of the pocket and reinserting it through the hole in the middle, back into play. I go on to concede a further four goals without reply. Andy tips his beer bottle to his mouth, draining the dregs before shaking his empty bottle at me.

'Loser buys,' he says, motioning towards the bar.

I turn and walk to the bar and order two of the draught lagers from South America that are currently on offer. The bearded bar man pulls the pump, sloshing some of the pale liquid over the edge. He wipes it with a cloth before pushing them towards me and taking my money. I walk back to the scene of my defeat, where Andy has chosen a nearby table. He thanks me for the pint and we both take a long pull.

'What do you reckon to Michael, then?' he asks, wiping his mouth with a napkin.

'He's an idiot who made a bad decision and is too much of an arse to admit it. He'd make a perfect politician. I think he is harmless, though. In the heat of the moment and in the excitement of receiving incriminating photos from an unknown source, pound signs flashed in his eyes and he didn't consider how far reaching the consequences of his action would be.'

'I agree,' he says. 'Do you really think he has no idea who sent the photos though?'

I nod.

'I think so. He has nothing to lose from telling us a source if he knew one.'

We descend into conversations unrelated to the case and I can feel the combination of the long day and the alcohol tugging at my eyelids. We decide to call it a night, exiting Café Kick and emerging onto Exmouth Market, a pretty street filled with boutique shops and looked over by twinkling fairy lights, suspended in zig zags above us.

The walk to the hotel is short. Before going in, I turn and take in the skyline of the capital. Red crane lights, high in the sky, dazzle like stars while the lead-covered dome of St Paul's Cathedral battles with The Shard for the title of the city's most impressive building. Old versus modern. Tower Bridge stands guard across the river, a rainbow of lights reflecting off the blackness of the water. It's an impressive scene.

My burning eyeballs plead with me to give them a rest, so I turn and enter the hotel. We take the lift to the fourth floor, walk to our respective doors and arrange to meet for breakfast, before bidding each other goodnight.

While I am brushing my teeth, I reflect on whether I'd one day like to join the Met. Try something new. This is probably only the third or fourth time I've been to the capital and I find myself wishing I had more time here to visit the landmarks and take in a theatre show. It might be nice for Leo to grow up with the options the capital affords.

But then, I think of the rolling hills just a ten-minute drive from my home in the North West and immediately, London feels imposing and vast. Too big. Too unmanageable.

I finish in the bathroom and make it to the bed. I'm out like a light before I know it.

THE HOTEL BREAKFAST is fine. I chase a sausage around the plate with a blunt fork while Andy rises for seconds. He comes back with another heaped plate, and I raise a castigating eyebrow.

'It's all-you-can-eat,' he says, spearing a sausage, its juices squirting as he bites into it.

'I don't think it's meant as a challenge,' I reply, setting my fork down with a tinkle on my plate. He shrugs and continues with the task at hand.

When he's finished, we walk to the front desk to check out. Andy rubs his stomach gingerly while I pay for the rooms. We navigate the city and arrive back at Euston with ten minutes to spare. Andy uses the time to go to the toilet while I peruse the magazines in WH Smith. I plump for a trashy mag with the pictures of Amanda and Eli on the cover, with promises of inside scoops, though I fail to see what some hack journo could have conjured up in the space of twenty-four hours that the police don't know about.

I meet Andy at the barrier, who is complaining about the price he's had to pay just to relieve himself, and we make out way onto the train, finding our reserved seats near the door. We slip into them with a contented sigh and push our bags underneath. A few minutes later, we pull away from the terminal and begin our journey north.

As we are passing through Stoke-on-Trent, my phone buzzes in my pocket. I expect it to be Tom returning my missed call from this morning, but it isn't. It's Angela at the station.

I answer with a cheery hello.

Her tone does not match.

'There's another body,' she says.

23

THE TRAIN PULLS into Stockport and Andy and I hightail it to the taxi rank, slipping into the back seat and telling him our desired location. In present company, we can't discuss the case, so we each get lost in our own thoughts and I prepare myself mentally for what is about to come.

Having grown up in Marple, I spent an endless number of hours hanging out in the Memorial Park during my formative years. We'd claimed the place as our own; drinking cheap cider by the basketball hoops whilst watching shirtless boys in the skate park, trying to impress us with tricks and failing miserably most of the time.

When the photo of Amanda and Eli was released, I'd known almost instantly where they were. Most of the park is wide open space, but there was one bench, dubbed the kissing bench, which was revered for its secluded location in a small alcove near the library. Beyond it, a dense woodland took over. Privacy is everything in a small village. The last thing you want when you're sucking face is your mum walking by on her way home from the shops. The unwritten rule was, those that were in a relationship had first dibs on the bench. Teenagers may be a disagreeable bunch, but that was one decree we all stuck to.

Like Fight Club for horny young lovers.

The taxi comes to a stop at the entrance to the park, which has been cordoned off to the public by the thin strip of tape blowing in the wind. We pay the driver and leap out of the car, running amongst the police cars and forensic vans in the library car park towards the alcove, Andy a few steps behind. The community police officer who found the body attempts a small smile, but I can tell that what she has seen has affected her badly.

She introduces herself as Lucy and points to the trees behind her, already a hive of activity.

'Before you go,' she croaks, 'that woman came forward when she saw the hoohah. Says she saw something.'

She points to a woman huddled under a spotty umbrella, who is sitting on a bench that overlooks the pristine bowling green. I weigh up what should come first – crime scene or possible witness - and Lucy seems to read my mind.

'She says she's happy to wait.'

Decision made, we make our way past her to the outer cordon and sign in to the crime scene, donning protective suits.

Martin and his team are in the process of erecting a tent over the body; to preserve the crime scene from the forecasted rain and also to keep prying eyes at bay. Another tent has been thrown up near the inner cordon, for discussions away from the body. Andy and I wait under this tent and watch Martin and his team of SOCOs comb the area around the body, not wanting to disturb the deceased until the forensic pathologist gets here. The team walk the wood in spaced lines, pausing every step to survey the area before taking another step, and repeating the process.

Half an hour later, John Kirrane joins us in the tent just as the rain starts to pour, running down the canvas roof like teardrops.

'No time like the present,' he says. We follow him and the crime scene photographer over the stepping plates laid out by the SOCOs and enter the smaller second tent. On the cold, wet ground lies the body of Eli Parker.

He is on his back. One arm is at a right angle to his body, the other bent at the elbow; his bloody palm resting on his chest. Dull, unseeing eyes point heavenward, his mouth open in a silent scream. His shirt has been ripped open down the middle. The warmth and boyish charm from the night I met him at the gig is gone.

In the hand of his extended arm is a lavender rose.

John takes his time circling the body, speaking into his voice recorder as he goes. Every so often, he asks for photos to be taken and checks the screen on the camera to make sure he has got what he needs. When he has finished orbiting, he performs the essential medical checks. He motions for us to approach the body, finally ready to discuss his thoughts.

He leads us to the head and points to left side of the neck. A number of thin knife wounds are visible, from which a vast quantity of blood has spilled.

'It seems to me he was upright when these wounds were inflicted,' he says, pointing to the initial downward trajectory of the blood.

'This one,' he says, pointing to a ragged gash just above his stomach area, 'I think was done whilst he lay here, judging by how much blood there is in the vicinity.'

'What about that?' I ask, motioning to a crude cut on his left pec. I move around the body to study it from the right way up. Two diagonal strokes and a horizontal one have been carved into Eli's chest, forming a rough capital A.

'It looks like the symbol for anarchy,' says Andy.

'That usually has a circle around it,' replies John, looking at the cut with narrowed eyes.

'Oh, you uncultured swine,' I say. 'It's the scarlet letter.'

'Isn't that a film?' Andy asks.

'Yes, based on a book of the same name,' I reply. 'Did you ever watch the film?'

He nods. 'All I remember is that Demi Moore had an awful British accent and took a lot of baths.'

'Jesus,' I mutter, shaking my head. 'In the film, as in the book, the main character is an adulterer. She has a baby with someone other than her husband and is forced to wear a scarlet A on her clothes for the rest of her life as a punishment.'

I look at the deep lacerations on Eli's chest and wonder how much pain he suffered as they were inflicted; revenge for something he'd done over seven years ago. A couple more logs get added to the fire burning within me; the absolute desire of catching Johnny Mayhem.

'You think it's him?' asks John.

'Look at that fucking rose,' I spit, pointing to the flower in Eli's hand. 'It can only be him.'

'Well,' says John. 'The rose thing is common knowledge now, isn't it? Any bugger wanting to make it look like Mayhem is behind this has the perfect weapon to frame him with.'

I make a mental note to check in with the team canvassing florists, to see if any progress has been made. I don't let John's words derail me, though.

'Firstly,' I continue, 'he pretty much vowed on camera that Duane would get his just desserts. Then, less than twenty-four hours after the photos of his wife having an affair are released, the guy in the photos is dead. Tack on to that, that the fucker hasn't been seen in a week, hiding away like vermin, and I'd say all signs point to dear old Johnny.'

We turn our attention back to the body. There is a silence which follows my angry outburst, which Andy eventually breaks.

'Which of the wounds was the killer blow?'

'I can't be certain until I open him up. But I think he would easily have bled to death from the neck wounds if the chest wound hadn't been inflicted. The A is solely for decorative purposes, though I think was inflicted whilst he was alive.'

Nothing more can be learned from the body until John performs the post-mortem tomorrow. I push open the tent flaps and head back in the direction of the library. I glance down at the ground and notice the little yellow evidence markers following track marks in the soil. Spinning round, I can see that they begin at the tent. I step over the plates and follow the tracks back to the edge of the trees, where the community police officer is still sitting on the bench.

'Do we reckon Eli was stabbed in the neck here?' I ask Andy, pointing at the alcove area. 'Then dragged to where he is now, and killed there if he wasn't dead already.'

Because of the rain, I can't be certain that blood has been spilled by the bench. I call Martin, who hurries over when he senses the urgency in my voice, and ask him to try and find out. He tells me brusquely that they were already on it, but barks for the tent to be erected over the bench area as quickly as possible. Two suited men set off at pace towards the vans.

'We'd best go see his wife,' I say to Andy. 'But first, the eye witness.'

24

I GLANCE OUT of the library window as the rain lashes against it and the wind threatens to shake the glass from its frame. The manager of the library has kindly given us use of her office to talk to the witness, as the biblical downpour had made being outside impossible. I worry about the loss of evidence from the crime scene below, and can only imagine the pressure Martin is putting people under to be thorough despite the deluge. The door clicks and the lady from the bench enters, having made use of the facilities before joining us.

She unwraps a silk scarf from around her neck and pulls her damp, grey hair into a ponytail. As she sits down opposite us, she takes her glasses off and wipes them on the bottom of her hoodie, in an effort to de-mist them. She reaches into her bag and pulls out a packet of mints. She slips one from the packet and pops it into her mouth, before offering us one, which we both decline.

I fish a notepad out of my bag and take a pen from the desk's stationery supply. Andy introduces us and tries to put her at ease. She tells us her name is Cathy and that she is happy to help in any way she can.

'Why don't you start by telling us what you saw last night?'

'Well,' she starts. 'I was walking in the park with my dog, Albert. He's old and he likes the same loop—it's a good length for him. We always pass the secluded bit and I usually smile as I get a peek of the lovers that think they are hidden away from the world. As we were passing last night, I heard crying, so I had a little look in.'

I brace myself. 'Did you see Johnny Mayhem?'

'Who?' she asks, her brow furrowed in confusion. 'It was a man and a woman. Older than the usual sorts you get in there.

The woman was holding a rose and the man was crying. When I told my husband about it later, he said they were probably splitting up. That the man had more than likely done something wrong, tried to make it up to her by giving her a flower, and then was surprised when that wasn't a grand enough gesture to keep her.'

I pull up a picture of Eli Parker on my phone and show her it.

'Was that the man?' I ask.

She takes the phone from me and holds it up close to her face, eyes squinting in order to scrutinise the picture.

'Yes, I think so,' she says, 'though I couldn't be 100% sure.' She pushes the phone across the table to me again, which I pocket before turning back to her.

'Can you describe the woman?'

'I didn't get as good of a look at her. I was more distracted by the crying man.' She pauses and to her credit, she looks like she is trying hard to pull any modicum of detail from the recesses of her brain that may help us. 'She definitely had dark hair, and was wearing a dark coat. But other than that, and the fact she was holding a rose, I can't remember.'

'Did she look masculine?'

She looks confused by the question.

'No dear, I wouldn't say so.'

We continue to probe her for information but it's clear the well is dry. She says that, aside from the brief conversation with her husband, she completely disregarded the event until she saw the police tape rolled across the entranceway to the alcove on her way to the library today, so made herself known to someone official. She apologises that she can't help more, and I assure her that she has been of more assistance than she can know. She leaves the room and we watch her disappear down the stairs through the frosted glass office windows.

'A woman did this?' Andy asks, and I put my head in my hands.

WHEN JANE PARKER opens the door, she is dressed head to toe in black, as if she had anticipated the outcome of the search for Eli when she chose her clothes this morning. Her dark hair hangs in waves, a fringe encroaching on her blotchy red eyes. It takes seconds before tears spill down her cheeks as she registers our solemn expressions.

'Oh, Jesus,' she mutters, pushing the door wide and allowing us in to her house, not needing to hear the words to know what has happened.

The front door opens onto a small square of hallway. Ahead are the stairs and to the left is a door that leads into a living room. Photos of Jane and Eli in happier times line the walls of the large room; a wedding day snap, a tanned Eli at a lakeside table, shoving pizza into his mouth. Andy and I take our places on the three-seater sofa opposite Jane, who has sunk into an armchair, her head in her hands. I take my notepad out and introduce myself.

'We're sorry to have to tell you, but Eli's body has been found.'

Huge, wracking sobs erupt from her and tears stream down her face. I pull a packet of tissues from my pocket and hand them to her. We leave her to her grief for a few minutes. I sit on the sofa, waiting for her, while Andy goes to the kitchen. I hear the running of water and the click of the kettle. After a few minutes, he emerges with a tray of mugs. He sets it on a sideboard and offers her one, which she declines.

'Mrs Parker… Jane,' I say. Hearing her name seems to calm her slightly. She sets the tissue on the arm of the chair and looks our way. 'Jane, we have a few questions. We're happy to wait until you are ready and can come back later, or tomorrow.'

She shakes her head. 'I'm ready.'

After checking that she is sure and assuring her that we can stop at any time, we begin.

'Can you tell us about last night?'

'Like I said on the phone earlier to whoever I spoke to in the office, we had a fight about the photos on the news. My father had an affair and I've always hated cheating. He'd told me in the past that he'd never cheated on anyone and then all of a sudden, there is photographic proof that he has. On the national fucking news…'

She trails off and snatches up her tissue again, blowing her nose noisily.

'Sorry,' she says, dabbing at her eyes. 'It was just a lot to take in. I felt humiliated. He said that he was young and impulsive when that happened, and that he is a changed man. My mother always said "Once a cheater, always a cheater," and it stuck with me. So, we argued about it. I asked him was he still with his first wife when he was sleeping with the model, and when he said yes, I told him to get out.'

'Do you know where he went?'

'No, I rang around all his friends and his family, but no one had heard from him. I told them all to let me know the moment they'd heard from him. I thought he might've checked into a hotel for the night. I checked our bank account online this morning but there were no outgoing payments.'

'Does he know anyone in Marple?' Andy asks.

'I don't think so,' she answers, confusion flashing across her features.

A memory from the night he spilled his drink over me suddenly resurfaces. I throw the words around in my head, trying to find a way to organise them so that they come out sensitively, but whatever order they come in, they're damning.

'Jane, did you attend a concert at the Apollo theatre on the evening of 21st November?'

'No,' she says, confusion etched on her face, 'but Eli did. He went with his brother'

'I know *he* was there; he spilled a drink on me.' I reply. I don't want to finish the rest of my testimony, but know that I have to. 'Jane, he wasn't there with his brother. When he spilled the drink on me, he bought me and my boyfriend another one, and said he was getting one for himself and his girlfriend.'

The hurt that washes over her face is painful to watch. Her eyes narrow for a second, and I think she is going to cry. Instead, she explodes out of the chair with a shriek and kicks over a table with a pile of books on it, scatting them across the floor. One of the wooden legs breaks off the table with a loud crack.

'That bastard,' she rages. 'That fucking bastard.'

She stands in the middle of the room, amid the debris of her anger, with her chest puffing and her hands balled into fists, as if challenging something in the room to make itself known to her ire. Andy and I watch her in silence and as her anger subsides gradually, she bends down to pick the books up, setting them on the sideboard beside the tray of cold teas.

'Sorry,' she says, still standing.

'I'm sorry that I had to tell you, but a witness saw Eli and a woman with dark hair last night in the Memorial Park in Marple last night. Do you have any idea who that might've been?'

'Dark hair?' she huffs. 'I should've fucking known. I'd put my house on it being Arabella Neale. They worked together and I could always tell he had a thing for her. He loved going to gigs and stuff like that and I was never that bothered, so he'd go to them with her. He always assured me that they were just friends who liked the same type of music and I foolishly believed him.'

'Where did they work?'

'It's a new bar in Romiley called The Treehouse. Fancy, hipster gins and what have you.' She suddenly clutches her hands to her face and wails about having to let his boss know what has happened.

While Andy tries to console her, I think about the possibility of it being Arabella that killed Eli. Maybe he called her for a shoulder to cry on after the argument with his wife. Maybe he called her to break up with her and she didn't like that. I make a note in my pad to call the bar and find out if Arabella was working last night.

'Do you know where she lives?' I ask, now that Jane has quietened down, but she shakes her head. There can't be too many Arabella's in Greater Manchester, so getting her address shouldn't be too much of a problem.

We thank Jane for her time and I promise to put a family liaison officer in touch with her, to help her with her grief. At the door, I throw one more question her way.

'You mentioned that Eli had been married before. Do you remember her name?'

She nods.

'Lyons was her maiden name. Susan Lyons.'

25

OUR CAR BUMPS its way down the narrow dirt track. It is barely wide enough for one vehicle. Overhanging, thorny branches claw at the dusty windscreen and thump off the roof. After a few minutes, we emerge from the tight lane into a gravelled drive.

The exterior of the farmhouse has seen better days. The weather-beaten walls are in need of some TLC and the wooden window frames, through years of expanding and shrinking to the merry dance of the elements, show draughty spaces between window and wall. The outside of the house belies what lies inside. The spacious living room that leads into a rustic kitchen with underfloor heating and a marble island. The playroom, Leo's favourite room, boasts sensory lights and all manner of baby toys. Whatever money has been spent has been on the practical, rather than the façade.

The sky overhead has calmed since this morning. The dark clouds have parted and moved on, leaving a cobalt blue in its place. Small wisps of white float lazily by. Susie is sitting on a picnic blanket near the front door with a book in her hand and a can of Diet Coke resting between her thighs. A pushchair is sat nearby, in the shade of a large conifer.

'Hello,' she calls, smiling, as we get out of the car. 'To what do I owe this pleasure?'

Andy and I take a seat on the picnic blanket beside her.

'It's not a personal call, I'm afraid.'

She looks confused.

'The body of Eli Parker was found this morning. He's been murdered.'

Her eyes widen and she scratches the back of her neck, letting the novel that was in her hand fall to the ground, the pages bending under the book's own weight.

'I'm sorry to have to be the one to tell you,' I say, 'but I didn't want you to find out on the news tonight. I think the chief is doing a press conference later this afternoon.'

'How did you know about us?' she asks, the tears brimming on her lashes.

'We've been to see his wife. After the photos… I assume you've seen the photos?'

She nods.

'After they were released, Eli and his wife had an argument. She was pissed that he'd cheated on you.'

A sad laugh escapes her mouth.

'It was never a proper marriage between us,' she says. 'Eli was from a very catholic family, though he had no interest in religion. We'd been dating for a couple of years and I got pregnant. He begged me to marry him, sharpish, so that we could say the baby was conceived within wedlock. His gran was ill and he didn't want to upset her so close to the end, so I agreed. We got married in Gretna. A shotgun wedding if you've ever seen one—the pictures are hilarious.'

The smile fades and melancholy replaces it.

'I had a miscarriage. And that was the end of us. We'd been growing apart, romantically, before the baby so it was probably for the best. We didn't have to stay together because of a mistake. We were in the middle of a divorce when he slept with Amanda.'

'Were you upset?'

'About him shagging around? Not in the slightest. We were trying to rush through the divorce. We were young. And I mean, have you seen her? I would've shagged her if she was that way inclined! Nah, we weren't involved romantically at that point, but we were still friends.'

Her light tone masks the sadness of the subject matter.

'I was upset about losing the baby—mistake or not. And I was upset last night when I saw the photos. If he'd told me at the time that he was seeing other people, I wouldn't have minded in the slightest.'

She glances over at the pushchair and I can feel the almost primal urge she's giving off, the need to go and hold her living baby tight to her chest, to feel the little fluttering heartbeats within the tiny chest.

'When did you last speak to Eli?' Andy asks.

Susie eyes him as if she has only just noticed that he is there. 'Probably about three years ago. I sent him a happy thirtieth text, but didn't hear back. I assumed he was living a happy life and didn't need a reminder from the past. I deleted his number after that.'

Andy scribbles in his notebook.

'Do you think it's him?' she asks, after a moment of silence. 'Mayhem?'

'We've got various lines of enquiry,' I say, hating myself for the fact that I can't tell my friend, my *grieving* friend, about the dark-haired woman and the lavender rose in Eli's hand.

'Do you think I'm in danger? If you made the link between Eli and me, do you think he might too?'

I assure her that, if it is Johnny Mayhem who is behind this, that she probably doesn't need to worry. His victims seem to be people who have wronged him in some way. Duane, letting him rot in jail for seven years before coming forward with the evidence that freed him; Simon having led the investigation that sent him down and Eli for having sexual relations with his model wife. Me, maybe, though Victoria has me covered with a partner who never leaves my side and some nocturnal babysitters to watch the house. I hand her the card that contains all of the ways of getting in touch with me, feeling slightly stupid in the process.

'I know you have my mobile number, but sometimes it's quicker to get me on the work one. If you feel unsafe at any stage, call me and I can arrange police protection.'

Andy and I stand to go. Susie gets up and hugs me tight, the floodgates opening on her grief. Her body writhes against mine, great sobs puncturing the silence. Gradually, they subside and she pulls away, wiping mascara from her cheek.

'If you want to cancel the playdate tomorrow, I don't mind,' I say.

She shakes her head. 'No, it's fine. Though, maybe we could have it at someone else's house. The thought of having to go shopping now is…' She trails off.

'We can do it at mine,' I assure her, and she smiles. 'But if you don't feel up to it, just let me know.' She gives me one final hug before I get into the car. There is a message from HQ, informing us of Arabella's address. Someone has checked with The Treehouse and confirmed that she was not on rota last night.

As we pull out of Susie's driveway, I can see her in the mirror, sat like a statue on the picnic blanket, cradling her sleeping baby in her arms with tears flowing down her face.

ARABELLA'S HOUSE IN the middle of Hyde is the complete opposite of Susie's. The new build's red brickwork is complimented by white painted window frames and a bright blue door, protected by a slanting canopy. It could've been built yesterday.

I ring the bell and listen to the jingle echo throughout the interior of the house. A key is inserted into the lock on the other side of the door, it turns with a click and when it swings open, a pretty woman with long, dark hair is standing in the doorway. Her hazel eyes are accentuated by smoky eyeshadow and a tight, black long-sleeved top shows off her curves. She greets us with a smile that shows off a row of perfect teeth.

There is something about her face that is recognisable, thought I can't place it.

Andy introduces us and she invites us in, a worried look etched on her face. She is biting her lip as she sits down on a chair in the living room.

'Do you know Eli Parker?' I ask, taking a seat on a cheap IKEA style sofa.

'Yes, we work together,' she answers, her voice shaky.

'At The Treehouse, is that correct?'

She nods her head and clears her throat.

'Did you ever hang out with Eli outside of working hours?' Andy asks.

'Sometimes. Not often, but yeah, sometimes.'

'Why?'

She looks confused by the question.

'Because we're friends. You spend that amount of time working together and you get close with people, you know?'

'Close how?'

'Friends close,' she answers, gauging the look on our faces. 'Oh, God, no, we've never been anything closer. He can be flirty when he has a drink, but he's got a wife and he's ten years older than me, so I could never see him that way.'

'Were you with him last night?'

'Yes, we went for a drink in Marple. He called me up saying he'd had another argument with his wife. Seems to be happening more and more regularly these days. Anyway, we went for a few cocktails. Actually, I had a mocktail because I was driving, but he got a bit merry. Tried it on a bit, but I told him to think about his wife. He got pissed at me and left. Left me to pay the tab and all.'

'Did you follow him?'

'No,' she says, shaking her head. 'I've never seen him like that. Obviously, with those photos and everything, I expected him to be angry, but not with me for knocking him back again. Anyway, I finished my drink, paid the bill and came home.'

'So, you didn't go to the park with him?'

She shakes her head. 'No, like I say, I came home. I had to walk that way, because I parked in the car park beside the post office, but I didn't see him again. Is he okay?'

'I'm sorry to have to tell you this,' I repeat for the third time today, 'but Eli's body was found this morning, in the woods in the Memorial Park.'

She clasps her hands to her mouth. We give her a few minutes to let the news sink in, before asking our final questions.

'Can anyone corroborate your story?' I ask.

'You don't… you don't think I have anything to do with it, do you?' she asks, tears springing to her eyes. 'I called my mum on the way home to tell her about Eli's behaviour and she told me to ignore him and to get home and have a bath.'

'But no one actually saw you come in?'

She shakes her head.

'No. Maybe someone saw me out the window, though. The 8 o'clock news was just finishing on the radio so it would've been around then.'

We thank her for her time and leave. Andy rings the station and asks for a few uniforms to knock on doors around her estate, in order to verify her story. He pushes his phone into his pocket and reverses out of the drive. I pull my own phone out and call the team outside Johnny Mayhem's house. The team have had no luck so far and there is talk of reassigning them. It's costly business to have skilled coppers sitting in a car, watching a deserted house for days on end.

Kyle answers.

'Anything?' I ask.

'We've been called to respond to an emergency not far away. Hit and run,' he says. 'Team one were due to take over in about ten minutes anyway and, to be honest, fuck all is happening or will happen at that house. Mayhem has gone to ground.'

I thank him and hang up, dialling the number for team one straight away. Panic blossoms in my chest, an instinct that something isn't right.

'Hello,' Gary answers, caught mid-chew.

'Are you at the house?' I ask.

'Just turning the corner now, we got slightly delayed,' he replies, and I can hear the guilt in his voice. 'It's not like anything will have change…'

He trails off.

There is a burst of swearing.

'Boss,' Gary says. 'His car is gone. He's been here.'

26

'HE CAN'T HAVE got far,' Andy says for the hundredth time.

We pull into a petrol station and he exits the car. Whilst he fills the tank up, I listen to the chatter on the radio. The hunt for Johnny Mayhem is well and truly on. As many patrol cars as possible are on the road and it feels like a matter of time before he is caught. The car he has chosen to drive isn't exactly inconspicuous. I hear Andy replace the pump with a rattle of metal and watch as he walks towards the double doors, into the shop to pay.

The radio crackles again, and a deep voice confirms that there is no sign of him in Denton so far and that they will keep looking.

I question his intentions. He can't just change the plates or get the car painted a different colour. The car is so rare that even if it suddenly turned red, we'd know it was him. Was his plan to escape the country before the alarm was raised? But surely if he'd chosen that exact moment, he must've known that his house was being watched. He could've been in one of the other cars parked along the road, keeping watch on the watchers.

The various ports around the country are in the process of being informed about the car, so that it and Johnny can be detained upon arrival, so that option has been taken away from him. So, what is he up to?

Suddenly, a roar sounds from the road. I imagine some dickhead on a motorbike, gunning it up the slight incline, but when I turn to look, it's him.

It's Johnny.

I climb across to the driver's seat and start the ignition, pulling up to the door of the shop. I watch Andy shout something to the employee and leave the line. He emerges from the door and runs to the car, jumping into the passenger seat. I accelerate away before he has even closed the door.

'It's him,' I say.

Because we are in an unmarked police car, I don't bother with the sirens or the lights. I want to keep him in my sights, without him knowing that we are tailing him, until we have back-up in the area.

Andy is on the radio, asking for assistance from whoever can provide it. Immediately, offers are made and Andy provides the location in real time, the handset held tight to his lips. He sounds like a rally driver's navigator. Control confirm that a helicopter will be diverted towards our area within minutes.

The hunt is on.

Despite the loudness of his car, he is driving at the speed limit, probably trying to blend in—as much as that's possible in the eye-catching car. We are a few cars back and I am confident he won't know that the police are on to him. Every turn he takes, we take too, always keeping a comfortable distance. The thought of the killer being in our reach is making my skin tingle, and I fight against my instincts to speed up and try to take him myself.

Softly, softly, catchy monkey.

Suddenly, though, I can hear police sirens.

So, it seems, can Johnny.

In a cloud of thick, dark smoke, the black car ahead of us pulls out into the fast lane and overtakes a number of cars. I accelerate to keep him in view, pushing the speed to just over sixty miles per hour whilst Andy hits the blues and twos. Johnny veers into the inside lane again and pulls the car into a tight left-hand turn, entering a narrow residential street. We follow him, though he is nearly at the other end of the street by the time we turn into the quiet road. He flies around the corner at the opposite end and disappears from view.

The radio crackles into life and the helicopter team confirm that they have eyes on our target and that they will continue to keep track of him. We whizz around the corner, just about catching sight of the car as it disappears over the brow of the hill. A different voice sounds on the radio. A traffic officer tells us that he is going to take over as lead chaser, and a minute later, a marked police car overtakes us, sirens blaring. We trail in its wake, hoping to be of assistance once the chase is over.

The black sports car swerves in and out of traffic at high speed before ploughing through a set of traffic lights, stopped at red. A cacophony of angry horns fill the air as the cars with the right of way brake and skid across the road, narrowly avoiding smashing into the rock star's black bullet. The stench of burning rubber fills our car as we navigate the tight gap.

Andy continues to monitor communication on the radio whilst all my concentration is focussed on the road ahead. I push the thought of crashing at high speed out of my mind and can already imagine Tom's angry words when I tell him what I've been up to today. The radio quietens and Andy relays the information.

'The chopper team reckon he's trying to head towards the Peaks. They've plotted the most obvious route and two ground teams are setting up stingers. First one is a mile and a half away.'

The road ahead narrows as we enter a small village. Cars indicate and pull into the relative safety of grass verges and bus stops as the convoy of destruction passes through, the speed not letting up. The picturesque church spire and the lonely village shop pass in a riot of colour as we exit the village onto winding country roads. A sign for another village is doused in blue light as we speed past.

'This is where the first stinger is,' Andy says.

The road is straight and stretches out of sight. I can see a pelican crossing in the distance and an island that separates the two sides of the road. I know that that is where the stingers will be laid out, awaiting our runaway. The moment Johnny notices the strip of metallic spikes designed to shred his tyres is obvious. The car veers to one side, attempting to avoid the spikes by going on the wrong side of the road.

But he's not quite fast enough.

The front tyre on the passenger side is caught by one of the spikes, causing the car to swerve over the road, narrowly avoiding the island and the set of traffic lights. Sparks fly as the rubber of the tyre shreds away and the metal rim of the wheel makes contact with the asphalt.

His speed takes a dip but his determination to outrun the police does not. He surprises everyone by taking a left back towards civilisation, away from the hills of the mountainous Peak District.

A blast of noise erupts from the radio as the second stinger team is told of his change of direction, rendering them useless. Hasty contingency plans are made, hope holding them together rather than any firm knowledge of what he's going to do next.

Despite the damage to the car, Johnny is in no mood to concede defeat. He flies through more traffic lights, unaware or uncaring of the risk he's posing as he defies the red lights. We approach a roundabout and at the last minute, he veers to the right, entering the junction in the wrong direction. Cars part in his wake and horns blare, combining with our sirens to suffocate the senses.

A transit van with ladders secured to the roof rack pulls out of another junction. There is no way he could be oblivious to the madness surrounding him, but he pulls out with a jolt anyway. His bumper collides with the right side of the sports car, knocking it off course. The rapidly disintegrating wheel mounts the sloped, black and white section of the roundabout.

It flies through the junction.

Because of the speed he is travelling at and the jerkiness of his steering, there is nothing he can do to avoid the grassy knoll. He careers over it at speed, turning in the air. The driver's side smashes into a thick oak tree with a sickening crunch.

The police car ahead of us navigates the hillock with precision, stopping when he has kissed the passenger door with his bumper, preventing Johnny from escaping the car from that side. As quick as a flash, the officer in the passenger seat is out and running to the sports car.

I park on the footpath and pull the handbrake on. The adrenaline pulls me from the car and I run at speed up the slippery grass verge and approach the crashed car. The police officers from the lead car have the scene under control. The suspect has been detained and the driver of the police car is phoning for an ambulance.

A thick fog of smoke billows from the crumpled bonnet and shards of glass litter the ground from the smashed rear window. An indicator blinks and teardrops of petrol drip onto the grass, coating the blades in an oily sheen. Anguished cries escape the interior of the car. It's then I realise that the screams are coming from the passenger's side, as well as the driver's.

One of the officers hops into their car and reverses slightly, giving access to the passenger's side of the sports car. I run to it and open the door. The terrified eyes of a young woman, partially obscured by a thick dark fringe, greet me. She's probably in her early twenties. I don't know yet in what capacity she has been involved, but I still pull her out of the car and cuff her.

I glance across at the driver's side.

The man's lips curl into a snarl.

'You bellend,' I say, as he is cuffed and led away.

27

THE DOCTOR FINISHES writing on the clipboard and secures it to the foot of the bed. He assures the slightly broken man lying on the bed that help is only a buzzer press away, nods a curt goodbye to me before squeaking off across the linoleum floor and out the door.

'Olly Pilkington,' I say, addressing the ginger, muscle clad figure on the bed. 'Why am I not be surprised?'

Olly Pilkington had been a suspect on the last case I worked before maternity leave. As leader of the Longsight Lunatics, he'd been suspected of the murders of rival gang members, but in the end, it hadn't been him behind the atrocities. Not all of them, anyway.

Olly had a reputation of worming his way out of trouble. He'd gladly throw someone under the bus if it meant he escaped any recriminations. Finally, he was going to be brought to justice.

'I'm going to ask you a few questions. Now, between you and me, you're fucked, right? You're going away for a long time. So, there's no point in the bullshit you usually spout. I want the truth.'

He smiles at me, exposing bloody stumps where his teeth have recently been knocked out. His nose has crumpled under contact with the steering wheel and broken legs hide under the soft bedding.

'What do you want to know?' he drawls, in a thick Mancunian accent.

'Let's start with how you came to be in possession of Johnny Mayhem's car, shall we?'

'I found it.' He laughs at his own joke.

In my head, scenes from Stephen King's Misery float by. I imagine exposing his shattered legs and going full Annie Wilkes on them, in an effort to wipe that smug grin off his face.

Instead, I smile back.

'And how did you find it?'

'Truth, yeah,' he says, like he's getting down to business. 'We've been staking that house out for weeks. That rock star clown is laying low, biding his time until he surfaces again to kill someone else. He ain't ever making it home. He's either going to jail when you lot get your finger out, or he's gonna die in the process. So, I thought the car should get some love.'

'You said you were staking it out?'

'Yeah. We took it in turns. Your fat officers started with good intentions, but they got sloppy. They'd take off early, leaving the house unwatched. A few of my fellas called in a fake emergency in the area. Your lads took off well before changeover time, and we knew the coast was clear.'

'And once you stole it, what was the plan? It's not exactly a car that blends in.'

'I hadn't thought that far ahead,' he laughs. 'All I wanted to do was have a drive around in it. I'd probably have taken it back, no harm done, if you lot hadn't got involved.'

He points to a cup of water on the bedside table. I reach across and pass it to him, though he doesn't attempt to take it from me. Instead, he opens his mouth in a tiny circle.

'I'm not doing that,' I say.

'Sorry, officer,' he replies. 'It's just, my throat is getting dry and I don't think I can answer any more of your questions.' He fakes a cough and fixes his eyes on me.

Shaking my head, I force the straw into his mouth and listen as he slurps up the cold water. He nods when he is finished, a sign that I should remove the straw. I replace the drink on the side and continue.

'Do you know Johnny?'

'Nah, man. We're from different worlds, him and me.'

'Who was the girl?'

He smiles.

'Ah, she's just my latest shag. Nowt serious.'

'As erudite as ever,' I say. 'Thanks for your time, Olly. Enjoy prison.'

I get up from the seat and walk into the corridor, alerting the officer outside the door that he should return to keep vigil in Olly's room. He gives me a *fuck you very much* look, before marching into the room. Andy is waiting for me by the reception desk. On the way back to the car, he tells me what he has gleaned from the girl who was with our gangster. He confirms that she was Olly's latest squeeze and that he told her they were just going out for some food. She got in the car because she was scared.

'Poor girl,' I say, as I duck into the passenger seat, having had enough of driving for one day. 'But, that's what happens when you get into bed with gangsters.'

THE ATMOSPHERE IN the briefing room is flat. The excitement of the Johnny Mayhem chase has given way to disappointment that it was not him behind the wheel, only a local thug that everyone hated.

That is the trouble with gossip and rumours. With getting yourself excited for no reason.

The room quietens as I walk to the front, knowing that everyone needs a shot in the arm. Unfortunately, instead of answers, I'm only going to pose more questions. Questions that, so far, we have no fucking idea how to answer. I steel myself for the frustration I'm about to cause. Frustration I feel myself.

I pull the case board into the centre. Someone has already attached a photo of Eli's body, laying on the cold ground, surrounded by trees. Another photo shows a close up of the puncture wounds on his neck and yet another displays the capital A, carved into his chest. Everyone in the room will have had a chance to study them, and I hope someone offers something of use.

'Right,' I say, wearily, opening the briefing. 'Developments.'

I tell the crowd of officers about the body. Where it was found, who it was and any information we have on him. I tell them about the witness who saw the victim sitting on the secluded bench with an unknown brunette. I tell them about his wife and how they had a fight that she would never get to make right, and about Arabella, with whom he had a drink not long before his demise.

Head scratching abounds.

'At least we have leads now,' someone says from the back.

Whispers become murmurs. A quiet flood of questions are thrown back and forth and I allow them to get it out of their systems before calling for their attention. I try to answer the questions that I have heard, though my patience is fraying.

'Here we go. No, we have not ruled out the wife. She fits the description of the brunette and does not have an alibi. No, we have not ruled out Arabella, the woman he had a drink with. She doesn't have a solid alibi either. In fact, we're waiting on CCTV from Marple high street to find out if she told us the truth about what happened between them.'

'And what about Johnny Mayhem?' a young officer asks, his eyebrows rising as if he's surprised the question came from his own mouth.

The million dollar question.

'Honestly? Who knows? There are three hypotheses. One, Johnny Mayhem is behind all of this. The threat against Duane in the documentary alongside the roses suggests his involvement.'

'Hypothesis two is that the mystery brunette is helping Johnny out—doing his dirty work. This would make sense— Duane might've thought he'd pulled, invited her back to his bedroom, when really, he was the one being targeted by her. Simon was waiting on a brunette to come to his house for a drink when he was clubbed to death. The witness from last night suggested Eli was crying so it could've been someone he was seeing behind his wife's back and was calling it off. Chances are, she killed him for Johnny.'

'And hypothesis three?'

Hypothesis three is the most unlikely. It is also the one that scares me the most.

'That Johnny Mayhem is not involved at all.'

A swell of noise erupts. Wild theories are thrown around and the level of noise increases as voices rise to be heard over one another.

What about his fingerprints on the gun used to kill Duane?

What about his phone being triangulated to the area where his drug dealer pal lived?

What about the roses? The pocket watch? The fact Eli had been fucking his wife behind his back?

It must be him.

That's what everyone keeps saying.

It must be him.

But, in my heart, I'm not so sure anymore.

This brunette has changed the whole landscape of the case.

Once everyone has had a chance to voice their opinion, the room becomes quiet again. Officers are assigned to various locations around Manchester. More feet on the street might put Mayhem under pressure if, indeed, he is our perpetrator. Someone must know where he is. More house visits are planned. More known associates are going to receive a visit from uniformed officers in the coming days. The squeeze is coming.

While the jobs are divvied up, I retreat to my office and write a list of what I must do next.

1. Get the CCTV footage from Marple high street to see whether or not Arabella was telling the truth.

2. Talk to Jane Parker again. A fight with her husband cannot be undersold. She was upset and most murders are crimes of passion. Unplanned. Unthought of until the red mist descends. And I saw the red mist descend for myself in her living room. Who knows what she's capable of?

3. Look over the case notes from Amanda Mayhem's murder again—perhaps there is something to be gleaned from them.

In his version of events, Johnny claimed to be somewhere else while Amanda was being killed. Maybe that *somewhere* is where he is now.

I tear the list from my notepad and am about to shove it into my pocket when I think of two more things.

4. Get in touch with Michael Sims again. With Eli's murder, Michael has blood on his hands and he should bloody well know it.

5. Call into Tesco on the way home to pick up supplies for the NCT meet up tomorrow.

I fold the piece of paper into my pocket, log off the computer and leave the room, the bulging document of Amanda Mayhem's murder held tight under my arm. As I walk towards the lift, I have two thoughts. One is of Leo's little face and how much I cannot wait to see it. The other is of Tom's reaction when I tell him about the car chase. I know he'll be furious that I was involved at all, and to tell him that I was behind the wheel would be like signing my own resignation. As the lift doors open and I step towards my fatigued reflection, I wonder how far I can bend the truth in my recollection of the day's events. I push the button and the doors slide shut, sealing the office off from my view.

The darkness of the evening is setting in as I reach my car. I set the Mayhem case file on the passenger seat, and marvel at how the world turns. In the afternoon, you're involved in a high-speed chase and in the evening you're trundling around a supermarket, grabbing items from the shelves for a small get together of new mothers.

It's a strange world.

28

'SO HE WAS pissed off?' asks Jill.

'Pissed off is an understatement,' I laugh, though the rage and disappointment that seethed from every pore of Tom's body when I told of my exciting day had been far from funny. It had unsettled me. I'd never seen such cold fury erupt from him before.

'I think it was badass,' says Susie. 'I can't believe it wasn't that fucker in the car though.'

For most of the day, she'd been down in the dumps; understandable after the news she had been delivered yesterday. Losing someone who played a part in your life is never easy, no matter the distance or time that had passed since they were deemed significant.

The morning passes in typical fashion; hungry babies are fed and stinky nappies are changed. Susie did not allow Eli's death to become an elephant in the room. She addressed it early, discussed how she felt about it and the matter was put to bed, though the sadness was there for all to see.

After lunch, the maelstrom of reclaiming toys begins. Jill shoves a plush elephant into her change bag, only to realise that it belongs to Annie's baby and that her own is a slightly deeper blue.

I think about how trivial all this is compared to catching a killer. As much as I love spending time with them, and how thankful I've been for their support, especially during those first few months, I just want to get on with work. An email had pinged on my phone just over an hour ago—the subject line telling me the CCTV from Marple precinct had arrived. Each second since had felt like an eternity, and as the women and their babies leave my door with promises of seeing each other again soon, my mind drifts to the contents of the recording.

After all the excitement, Leo quickly falls asleep in his cot and I make my way quietly downstairs. I open the laptop and find the email.

Ross Powell, sender of footage and technological wizard, has written a short message.

I've pieced Arabella's journey together for you from the CCTV available. Hope it's helpful.

I make a cup of tea while the footage downloads, tapping my fingers impatiently on the table while watching the blue spiral curl around, almost making a circle to signal that the download is complete. When it does, a window launches and I'm transported to the inside of a bar I know well.

The footage is shot from a camera above the entrance. The room is narrow and the space houses six booths, back-to-back, along one side of the wall. Along the other wall is the bar, whilst the wall space above is taken up by framed paintings from local artists.

Eli is sitting in the booth at the back when Arabella walks in. Despite being *'just friends'* with Eli, she has gone to some effort for their meeting. Her dark hair has been straightened, her perfectly straight fringe just covering her eyebrows. Her toned midriff is exposed and tight jeans hug her curves.

She must've started getting ready as soon as she received his call. No-one dresses like that for a lonely, lazy night in front of the television.

They talk, though there is no sound on the video, and Arabella slips into the booth while Eli walks to the bar. He returns a few minutes later, with a couple of drinks in hand. A pint for him and a fruity cocktail, complete with tiny umbrella, for her, though she did tell me it was a non-alcoholic one.

They converse for a while before Eli goes and gets another round. He downs his pint pretty quickly and reaches across the table, his hand settling on Arabella's. She withdraws it as if she has been scalded, and shakes her head. He tries touching her face, but she pulls away from him and says something. He stands up, gesticulates angrily with his hand before stalking down the narrow bar and leaving.

Arabella stays sitting for a few minutes, her shoulders visibly rising and falling before slipping out of the booth. She glances back and notices something on Eli's recently vacated seat. She grabs it and walks the length of the room, paying at the bar on her way out.

The screen changes to show the street outside. At first, Eli walks up the cobbles. His journey takes him from the bar to the entrance of the Memorial Park, where he would later meet his end. He walks through the archway and disappears from view.

Arabella's journey is shown next. She walks with purpose, a jacket in her hand. Presumably the one Eli left behind. She gets to the crossroads at the top of the town. Right leads her to the car park near the post office where she left her vehicle; to where she told us she went straight after leaving the bar. Left leads to the park. The park she categorically denied going to.

Her head turns right.

But only for a second before her body turns left. She looks up and down the street and waits for a car to pass, before crossing the road and entering the park through the same archway as Eli had.

So, she lied to us.

The timestamp shows that she entered the park ten minutes after Eli did. The footage begins to speed up. Couples walk past the entrance to the park, hand in hand, and cars whizz by. The footage slows again and for good reason.

Thirty minutes after entering the park, Arabella leaves again. She glances across the road and crosses when it is safe to do so. She peeks back over her shoulder as if she is afraid something or someone might be following her.

It's then I realise that she is no longer carrying the jacket.

WE DRIVE INTO the car park and get out. From the outside, The Treehouse looks inviting. Smooth rendered walls, floor to ceiling windows and a metallic cut-out of a tree above the door give the bar a modern feel.

Inside is more of the same.

The stone floor, polished oak bar and framed works of art on the wall lend the place a sophisticated air. Ornate bottles of gins from around the world line the shelves on the wall behind the bar, whilst craft ales with quirky names and distinctive pump clips are spaced at regular intervals along the wooden surface. Aside from a couple of people nursing pints at a table near the back of the room, we're the only ones here.

A man in a black shirt with a silver tree embroidered on the chest pushes through a door behind the bar and apologises for keeping us waiting when he sees us.

'What can I get you?' he asks. 'I can recommend the Magic City gin. Notes of juniper, citrus and vanil…'

'We're not here for a drink, actually,' Andy says, cutting him off.

The man grunts, disappointed at having his sales pitch interrupted.

'Is Arabella Neale working today?' I ask.

The man behind the bar nods.

'She's just out the back, having her break. I'll go get her for you.'

He disappears through the same door and a few minutes later, reappears with Arabella in tow. From the colour of her face and the expression she fixes us with, I'd say she knew who was waiting for her. She must've recognised us from the barman's descriptions.

'Arabella, we need you to come with us to answer a few more questions. We trust that won't be a problem?'

'Am I under arrest?' she stammers.

'No, we could just do with combing through some of the information you told us last time we met.'

The barman tells Arabella he will cover for her. She thanks him, hugs him and pushes up a section of the wooden bar, before following us to the police car. On the way to the station, she keeps her head down and remains quiet for the duration of the journey, only breaking the silence to thank Andy for opening her door once we've reached our destination. We lead her through reception and into the lift, which rises quickly to floor three, where we exit. I instruct Andy to take her to one of the interview rooms whilst I go to my office to pick up a few things. When I meet them in the interview room, Arabella is already sitting with her legs crossed and a solemn expression on her face. Andy presses a few buttons on the recording console and then takes his seat. I close the door and sit down beside him.

'Water?' I offer.

Arabella nods. I pour a small amount into a plastic cup and push it across the table towards her. She takes a sip before replacing it on the table.

'Interview with Arabella Neale commencing at six-thirty pm. Present are DI Erika Piper and DS Andy Robinson. She has declined the presence of legal aid.'

I take a sip from my cup.

'Arabella, we have some follow up questions. Can you please relay your version of what happened on the night of 27th November?'

Arabella tells the story of the night Eli and her had drinks, almost word for word from when Andy and I heard it previously. She has obviously rehearsed it well.

'Thank you,' I say, when she has finished. From a plastic wallet, I pull a number of photographs. Screen shots from the CCTV. I set them on the table in front of her, slowly, letting each image sink in.

The first image is of Arabella at the crossroads of the Memorial Park and the Post Office car park. The next is her crossing the road, copying Eli's steps towards the park. The third is of her leaving the park, the time stamp circled in fluorescent yellow highlighter.

'Okay,' she says, panic in her voice. 'I know how it looks, but I can explain.'

'It best be good,' Andy says. 'Because by lying to the police in the first place, it tells us that you've got something to hide.'

'Eli had left his jacket in the bar. I picked it up and was going to return it. That's all. I walked after him into the park, but couldn't see him, so left with it still in my bag.'

'Did you search for him, for...' I make a big deal of checking the time stamps on the pictures of her entering and exiting the park, 'thirty-three minutes?'

'No,' she says, shaking her head. 'It's not like that. I walked up to the skate park in the middle. You get a pretty decent view of the whole place and I didn't see him anywhere, so I sat on a bench near the canal and had a smoke. It was a nice evening and I had nowhere to be.'

'So, why did you tell us that you went straight home when we questioned you the other day?'

'Honestly, I was scared. The truth is, Eli and I did sleep together. Just the once, but even that is one time too many. Our boss paid for us to have our Christmas party in a hotel in Cheadle. We joined up with a few of the other pubs in Romiley and hired a function room. The boss also paid for us to stay over. Eli and I had too much to drink and I ended up in his room. When I woke up, I was devastated. Things hadn't been the same between us since. I thought if you knew we'd had sex, you might think I'd done it. You don't, do you?'

Andy and I stare back at her, stony faced.

'Miss Neale, when I was looking through another bit of CCTV footage, you appeared.'

I take an iPad from my bag and press play on the video. The footage of Duane and Johnny squaring up to each other plays out as before, and ends with Glenn and a brunette woman, holding a blonde wig, exiting the frame.

'That's you, isn't it?' I ask.

She nods.

'And you go by the name of Bea when you work at Havana?'

She nods again.

'Everyone used to call me Bella, which eventually got shorted to Bea. Arabella sounds so bloody pretentious.'

'Did you go home with Johnny that night?'

'No,' she squeals. 'I've gotten to know him these past months and he's been cool to me.'

'So, what happened when you chased after him?'

'He walked outside towards a taxi. When he opened the door, a woman ran up to him. They talked for a few seconds and then they both got in the taxi.'

'Could you describe the woman?'

She shakes her head.

'It all happened so quickly. She was taller than him, that's all I remember thinking.'

I pull out a still from the CCTV of the night Duane died. It shows the drug dealer and the woman sitting opposite me glaring at each other, having exchanged words.

'So, you know Johnny and Duane. And, from the looks of it, you had a problem with Duane. Can you tell us what the angry exchange was about?'

'Honestly,' she says, shaking her head, 'I can't remember the actual words. He was drunk and trying to score free shots, but I work on commission. He said some nasty stuff and I told him where to go.'

'Do you use a dating app currently?' I ask, changing the direction of the interview.

Her brow furrows in confusion and she nods.

'So, you have a possible link to all three victims,' Andy states.

Arabella's eyes fill with tears and she begins pleading her innocence.

29

'IT WAS ALL very circumstantial to be fair to the prick.'

Andy's parting words echo around my head as the motorway opens up before me and I push my foot down, letting the anger out on the tarmac. A court appointed lawyer had appeared shortly after Arabella had been placed under arrest. He laughed at the flimsy evidence we'd presented and dismissed it straight away.

In hindsight, arresting her had been a foolish thing to do. Rather than show our hand and leap at the first person who fits our outline, we should've put a case together to use when the time was right. Arabella had been waiting outside the police station for a taxi when I'd been leaving. An offer of a lift home stuck on the tip of my tongue, before realising how inappropriate that was. Just because we couldn't prove her guilt now, doesn't mean she isn't behind all the recent deaths.

The taxi had pulled up as I had driven off. In the mirror, I could see Arabella gesticulate to the driver before sloping into the back seat. The roar of the taxi's engine sounded as it pulled away from the kerb. We'd travelled in the same direction for a while before I lost sight of it in the busy motorway traffic.

After that, I'd gone home; slept, showered, eaten and got dressed for the day ahead. Now, we are on our way to Jane Parker's house for a few follow up questions. My phone rings and when I answer, Glenn Lumb's sleepy voice rings out over the speaker system.

'How do?' he says.

'Hi Glenn,' I reply, my eyes on the road. 'I was wondering if you could help me out with something.'

'Sure thing.'

I tell him about the video I had stumbled across on YouTube. The one where he tells the person behind the camera that he *knows things* about Mayhem that don't make for nice listening. To my surprise, he laughs heartily.

'That video was taken years ago when I was still getting fucked up on anything and everything that I could get my hands on. Like I've said before, the only thing the Johnny ever did to me was cut me adrift. He took my dream away from me when he fell in love. To be honest, when he wasn't acting the rock star and before he met *her*, he was a decent guy.'

After a few more minutes of small talk, I hang up and concentrate fully on the road.

'You're starting to doubt yourself, aren't you?' Andy asks. 'You don't think it's him anymore.'

I grunt a non-committal answer. The truth is, I haven't got a clue what to think. It feels like my thoughts are being pulled this way and that by invisible hands, leaving me frazzled and unable to focus on the bigger picture. Thankfully, we reach the turn for Jane Parker's street before I have to elaborate on my grunt.

Eli's widow welcomes us in silently and we follow her to the living room once more. She introduces her sister, who sits on the floor holding a pair of knitting needles. She smiles briefly at us before turning her attention back to her wool. We retake the places from our previous visit and I take out my notepad, reacquainting myself with the notes I'd made on our last visit here while Andy thanks her for seeing us.

'Hopefully we won't take up too much of your time,' I say. 'We just have a few follow-up questions.'

She nods her head wearily at me, before taking a sip from her glass of water. The bags under her eyes hint that she may not have slept much since finding out about her husband's infidelity and subsequent death.

I hand her a few printouts—a picture of Duane and another of Simon.

'Do you recognise either of these men?' I ask.

She holds up the picture of the drug dealer.

'Isn't he the chap that provided the evidence that freed Johnny Mayhem from prison?'

I confirm that she is correct. She studies the other picture but comes up empty.

'Have you seen any of these men in real life before?'

'No,' she says, looking at her watch and probably wondering why we are wasting her time.

I collect the pictures from her and try to work out how to word my next question without winding her up.

'Mrs Parker, could anyone confirm that you were at home on the night of the 27th November?'

'The night Eli was murdered, you mean?' she spits as her face reddens. 'You honestly think I had something to do with it?'

Before I can answer, Jane's sister discards her knitting on the floor and stands up.

'You can't seriously think that Jane has anything to do with this. She was the one that called the police, sick with worry. Now, unless you have any sensible questions for her, I'd suggest knocking it on the head before we put in a complaint about harassment.'

For a slight woman, she is fairly intimidating.

I mutter something about having to check all bases before thanking a sobbing Jane for her time and retreating to the safety of our car.

'That went well,' says Andy, as he belts up.

'At least we can rule her out now,' I reply, sarcastically.

I AWAKE WITH a start to a cry in the darkness. I wipe the sleep from my eyes and check the time. It's just past two in the morning. The glow from my phone screen shows Tom asleep, turned to face the wall. The shriek from Leo's room forces me out of bed and downstairs to heat up a bottle of milk. Once ready, I trudge upstairs and into the baby's room. I pull Leo out of the cot and onto my lap, pushing the teat of the bottle into his mouth, hoping the warm drink will quell his hunger and lull him back into sleep's embrace.

Leo gives a thankful burp as he finishes draining the bottle and snuggles into my arms. As tired as I am, these little moments will be the ones I look back on and cherish. I'm reluctant to put him back in his cot, but with a looming alarm, needs must. As I push myself out of the rocking chair, a creaking noise from downstairs interrupts the stillness of the night. A dull thud from the hallway and the slap of metal on metal tells me that something has been posted through the letter box.

Definitely not Royal Mail at this time of the night.

I set Leo carefully onto his mattress and pull his covers over him, before tip-toeing out onto the landing. The silence is disconcerting. In the darkness, I imagine the barrel of a gun, stuffed through the letterbox waiting for me. Instead, as I descend the stairs, all that greets me is a solitary envelope.

I turn it over to find only my first name scribbled on the front. I hook my finger under the flap and loosen it at one end, taking care not to rip it. When it is open, I peer inside, though can't make out its contents.

I push open the door to the living room and close it behind me again before flicking the light on. I turn the envelope upside down and stand transfixed as rose petals float to the floor. The envelope slips from my fingers and falls to the floor too.

I stare at the lavender rose petals for some time, unable to move, rooted to the spot.

I realise that I should put the petals back into the envelope. The forensics team might be able to get some finger prints off them, though the chances of that are slim at best. Whoever delivered them chose a time they assumed would allow them to shove it in the letterbox and slip away into the night, unseen. I imagine they also took the precaution of wearing gloves.

I grab for the envelope and notice something else. On the inside flap, there is some writing, scribbled in the same lettering as my name on the other side. The words send a chill up my spine.

I don't want to kill a serving police officer, but I will. Get off the case, Erika Piper.

Next to the words is a smudged fingerprint, and I can guess who it belongs to.

VICTORIA LOOKS AT me with concern etched on her face.

I reach into my bag and find the envelope, wrapped in a sandwich bag to help preserve as much as the evidence as possible. I explain about the midnight mail, its contents and my suspicions about the sender.

'I completely understand if you want off the case,' she says. 'In fact, perhaps it would be the best...'

'No,' I say, 'please don't take me off it.'

'But...'

'Look, it's only a threat, but whoever sent this is not about to kill a police officer. As long as I'm working, it's one more thing they've got to keep an eye on. The more distracted they are, the more chance we have of them slipping up.'

'Them,' she says, studying me. 'You're saying them and not him. You don't think this was Johnny?'

'No,' I say, sure for the first time that Johnny has not been behind any of this.

'Explain,' she replies.

'I'd rather give myself a bit of thinking time first, if that's okay? I have a couple of phone calls to make and a few things to look over.'

I look at her hopefully and she rubs her eyes, nodding. She takes the envelope from me and tells me she will send it to the tech team to see if there is anything to be gleaned from it. She assures me, against my protests, that she will bollock whoever was in the unmarked police car outside my house last night for not doing their job.

She tells me to be careful and excuses me, and by the time I've reached the door, she is already on the phone to the tech team explaining about my delivery.

30

AFTER LEAVING THE police, Simon Black went on to have a succession of jobs that never really stuck. He'd tried his hand at being a bouncer but had felt powerless at dealing with the drunken bellends who he'd regularly come into contact with. He'd then moved onto working as a maintenance man; mainly gardens, but the work was sporadic and required a certain level of knowledge about gardening. Again, it was never going to work out. His longest, and most recent, place of employment had been at a builder's merchants called Bricks. Unimaginative name, but it sold what it said on the sign, and more besides. The shop also doubled as a local builder's headquarters.

We pull into the quiet car park. Only a few heavy-duty vehicles are parked here, though they take up more than one space each. The tarmac is uneven. Deep holes are filled with murky water and Andy and I skirt around them, keen to avoid soaking our feet.

The shop is quiet inside. A huge man with hands like dustbins is deep in conversation with the casually dressed employee behind the counter. The till rings and the man reaches into one of the many pockets in his trousers and pulls out a wad of notes, peeling a few off and handing them across the counter.

A crash, followed by several loud swear words, sounds from the back of the shop. The man at the counter laughs and collects his things, leaving the employee free to assist with whatever has happened to the clumsy sod, who is still cursing, though at a reduced volume.

A stocky man with annoyance etched across his face stalks out of a back office for a better look at whatever has disturbed him. He tuts as he cranes his neck for a better view around the aisles, before deciding it's not worth any more of his time and only then does he notice us. Immediately, his annoyance is replaced with a wide smile. Tough, weather-beaten skin is stretched as he bares brown teeth, stained from years of nicotine use. A thick, dark moustache lines his top lip.

'How can I help you?' he says, addressing his question to Andy.

Typical, I think.

I introduce myself and Andy before my partner has a chance to open his mouth. I unfold a piece of paper and show him the picture of Johnny Mayhem, keen to make sure he is ruled out before the real work begins.

'This guy been in?' I ask.

'Johnny?' he says, nonchalantly. 'All the time?'

My heart skips a beat and my mouth dries up.

'Yeah,' he continues. 'Him, Freddie Mercury and Hendrix make up the Thursday poker game.'

He starts to laugh but quickly wilts under the weight of my stare. I tell him that we'd like to look through his business records, because we think it will help us with a case we are working on. The man tells us his name is Gary Lawson, and nods frantically at our request. He is still nodding, though slower now, as he leads us into an untidy back office. He apologises for the state of it and hurriedly pushes some paper into piles, keen to clear an area for us.

He excuses himself and walks into a side room, lined with bookcases. Box files with dates scribbled on their sides in thick black marker fill the shelves.

'How far back do you want to go, love?' he shouts.

He retrieves the files from my chosen dates and sets them on the table in front of us, one stacked on top of the other.

'You fancy a cuppa?' Gary asks, and we place our orders.

He returns a few minutes later, setting two steaming teas in chipped mugs in front of us.

'We shouldn't be too long,' I say.

'You take your time, love. I'm off to a job now, so if you can just leave the stuff there when you're done, Junior out front will file it away again. If you need to photocopy anything, there's one in there,' he says, pointing to a door beside the room with all the files.

He waves us goodbye and we settle in. Andy lifts the top file and opens it with a quiet click. I take the bottom one and do the same. It doesn't take long to find what I'm looking for. I run my hand down the side and find the corresponding date. The work had been booked a week before Simon Black was murdered, and cancelled a few days after.

I talk Andy through my theory, but he looks unconvinced. Spoken aloud, it sounds speculative at best, but I'm eager to show him that it is just one part of the puzzle.

'Should we pay a visit?' he asks, as we get back into the car.

I shake my head.

'No, I don't want to fuck this one up. Let's get the whole picture together, then make our move.'

THE REST OF the day is spent plotting. I wheel the case board into my room and strip it, keen to start again with fresh eyes; unblinkered by Johnny Mayhem.

I start by pinning up pictures of the three victims; Duane Miller, Simon Black and Eli Parker. Three men, unrelated except for the fact they were all known to Amanda Parker. Duane and Simon had a connection to Johnny, but Eli was unknown to the rock star.

The partially ripped condom wrapper at Duane's should've been the first clue that all of this death was at the hands of a woman, but the bigger picture hadn't been clear yet. The unopened prosecco and the two glasses at Simon's house were another push in the right direction. Finally, a positive ID that a visibly upset Eli had been talking to a dark haired woman on the bench where he had died.

Then the letter.

Why would someone send me the letter?

Most crimes are committed for money, love or revenge.

The crimes committed, in my opinion, don't fit any of these. The crimes committed in this case were for another reason entirely.

Covering their own arse.

Whoever is committing these crimes has a lot to lose, and so is doing something about it. Whoever killed these three men also killed Amanda all those years ago. And I think I can prove it now. I call Andy in and run my theory past him.

He still looks uneasy.

'It's good,' he says. 'But, there's just not enough evidence. I think if you take it to the DCI, she'd say the same thing.'

I know he's right, but it still pisses me off.

'I agree,' I sigh. 'Well, if it's evidence we need, let's get it.'

I excuse Andy and pick up the phone. I reach into my bag and retrieve my purse, pulling out a card with a telephone number on it. It answers on the third ring.

'Hello,' the voice says, unenthusiastically.

'Michael, it's Erika Piper. You know that you said if you could help out in any way, you would…'

'Well,' the television presenter interrupts. 'I said that… what I meant was…'

'I need you,' I say, deciding the best way to get what I want is to stroke his massive ego. 'Your involvement could help bring Eli Parker's killer to justice. Wouldn't that be worth it? Imagine the publicity after that—everyone would love you. Villain to hero.'

Silence falls between us.

'I know what you are doing,' he says. 'But you do know how to play to me. As long as you can guarantee it will be safe, I'm in.'

We briefly discuss the time scale and he agrees that he can make it north tomorrow. It doesn't give us much time to get everything in place, but it gives the killer even less time to put a plan together of their own. I thank him and as I am about to hang up, he asks one last question.

'I assume this has been okayed by your boss?'

I assure him that it has, and that everything is in hand.

'ABSOLUTELY NOT,' thunders DCI Killick. 'Can you imagine the beating the press would give us if anything were to happen to him. Yes, he's not exactly David Attenborough, but if anyone in the media found out that we were using a celebrity as bait for a killer, well...'

She trails off. I'd expected some resistance and had put a plea together in my head, hoping I wouldn't need it but knowing that I would.

'I think it's the only way of bringing the killer into the open. At least, this way, it's on our terms. It would be in a controlled environment, with our best people there. I've already spoken to the manager of the club and Michael, and they are both up for it.'

The *controlled environment* point had barrelled into her resolve like a body blow from a heavyweight, leaving her wide open. I go for the jugular; an uppercut of pure, unadulterated persuasion.

When I finish my final point, she sits quietly, deep in thought. I can see that the idea of having the killer in custody in the next twenty-four hours is swimming before her eyes. She sighs deeply.

'I don't like it,' she says, and my shoulders slump. 'But, if we can catch this bastard, then it's worth the risk. Call a team meeting.'

I pump my fist.

'But,' she warns me. 'At the first sign of trouble, you get him out. And if anything happens, know that you are coming to the guillotine with me. It's both our heads on the line.'

Fifteen minutes later, the briefing room has been filled. Killick says her piece, underlining time and time again how risky this is and how much is on the line for everyone. Then, she passes the floor to me and the planning begins. For the next few hours, ideas are discussed and then concreted into place. Set in stone. By the time the last person has walked out the door, everyone knows their role. A good night's sleep is ordered.

Tomorrow is going to be a big one.

31

MICHAEL SIMS EMERGES from the underpass linking Stockport train station with its small car park. Only, I have to look a couple of times to check it is him. Instead of his usual suit and tie, he's dressed in what can only be described as undercover chic.

A green Oakland A's baseball cap has been pulled low over his face and sunglasses obscure his eyes, despite the heavy rain. Stylish ripped jeans, a cashmere jumper and walking boots complete his strange look. Perhaps in downtown Los Angeles he might fit in, but in Stockport, he sticks out like a sore thumb. Behind him trails a suitcase on wheels—one that looks like its holding enough clothes for a fortnight abroad. He's only here for one night!

I get out of the car and wave at him. He flashes me a look that suggests that with the wave of my hand I've sentenced him to certain death. He freezes on the spot and looks around the underpass at his fellow arrivals. Seemingly happy, he stalks over to the car. Andy pops the boot for him and he drops his case in, the suspension groaning under the weight. He slams the boot door and races into the back seat. I raise an eyebrow in his direction before retaking my place in the passenger seat.

'Waving isn't very covert, is it?' he asks, throwing his cap onto the seat beside him and hooking a leg of his sunglasses onto the neck of his jumper.

'We don't think the mafia are on to your visit,' I laugh. 'You're safe.'

'For now,' he mutters.

The journey from the train station to the police station doesn't take long, though we are held up slightly by traffic on the ring road. A lorry with smoke billowing from it proving to be the hold up.

'A bad omen,' I hear Michael whisper from the back seat.

I roll my eyes.

When we get to the station, he emerges from the car with a raincoat on and a different baseball cap pulled over his head—this one bearing the purple and white of the Minnesota Vikings. He casts a glance around before following Andy and I into the building, hunched low like he's trying to avoid enemy fire. Once inside, his shoulders sag with relaxation, though he is still on edge. He nearly jumps out of his skin as the lift pings to signal its arrival.

We shuffle in and make our way to the third floor, where I lead him to my office. He collapses the handle of the suitcase and sets it by the door, before taking a seat in front of my desk. He pulls a silver hip flask from his coat pocket and unscrews the lid, taking a few hits with an expression that suggests he doesn't normally drink whatever is inside it. He slips the hipflask back into his pocket. From how quickly he chugs from a bottle of water to get rid of the taste, I don't think the hipflask will be seen again.

'Okay,' he says, replacing the lid. 'Tell me what I need to do.'

DCI Killick appears at the door as I start my spiel.

'You are going to have a lovely night out, all expenses paid, on us. You mentioned before that you had a few friends in the area that could accompany you?'

'Sean and Dan,' he confirms.

'So, you'll meet up with your mates and head to the club. I saw your Twitter post last night saying that you'd be in Havana tonight, so hopefully that should lure whoever is behind this out. At some point, probably towards the end of the night, they will attempt to make contact. We have been trying to think about what they might do, and we think they'll probably try to get you to take them back to your hotel. Let it happen, and we'll be outside to intercept.'

He nods, though his skin has paled somewhat. Despite having used words like *whoever is behind this,* the meaning is not lost. Whoever is behind this has killed three people recently. That's not something to be trifled with.

'We have a team in place—you won't be in there alone. They'll be disguised as revellers. You won't be able to tell them apart from the actual party goers, but you're safe in their hands. You'll be wired up so any conversations you have are recorded. I'll be in the office watching on CCTV. Any sign of trouble and we get you out. Any questions?'

'Where is the toilet?' he asks.

When he returns, his face grey and his eyes bloodshot, I hold up two pictures. The two women we think it could be. I make him study them, telling him that the hair will probably be different on account of the wig. He asks can he keep them so that he can have a proper look once he's had a sleep at his hotel. He pockets them and we leave the station again.

The journey to the centre of the city is slow, on account of Manchester City's home fixture. When we arrive outside, Andy finds a parking bay and waits in the car while I accompany Michael inside.

He barely pays attention to the beautiful façade of the Stock Exchange Hotel, the original copper-plated sign harking back to days of actual financial trade. The smartly dressed doorman nods a subtle greeting and pulls the door open for us. The finer details may be lost on my guest, but not on me. The reception area is stunning—the checkerboard flooring, the circular diamond chandelier and the marble pillars welcome you in style. History is told on the walls—framed photographs, stretching back over one hundred years, of moustached men in belts and braces, talking business around tables laden with glasses line the area behind the sleek reception desk.

We check in with a well-groomed man, who passes us a key card and offers to lead us to our room. We decline his offer, not bothering to correct his wrongful assumption that we are together, and walk up the stairs to the first floor, where we find his room at the back of the building. The key card turns the light on the handle from red to green and the door clicks open, revealing an opulent room.

He sets his suitcase against the wardrobe and sits on the plush bed, while I remain just inside the door. Worry is splashed all across his face.

'Get a few hours' sleep,' I tell him. 'Then get your mates round and have a drink. Not many, mind. We need you on your game and the minibar's prices are extortionate.'

My attempt at levity falls flat.

'Is this going to work?' he asks.

'Get some sleep,' I say, by way of reply.

He closes the door behind me and I walk back to the car.

'You should see in there,' I say, as we pull away from the kerb.

'I'm a Liverpool fan and that place is owned by two ex-United players. I shall never set foot in there as long as I draw breath,' he replies.

ROSS POWELL IS looking at the computer system in Havana's back office as if it has offended him. He shakes his head and mumbles to himself as he lifts cables, checking where they are plugged into and what purpose they are serving.

'This won't do,' he says dramatically. 'It's like trying to do an F1 race in a Fiat 500.'

I have no idea what he means, but I nod like I do. He tells me that he has some equipment to install before tonight, and waddles out the door, tearing the wrapper off a bar of chocolate and muttering about needing all the energy he can get.

Now alone in the office, I check the bank of screens showing the interior of the club. With the lights on, the cameras have access to every nook and cranny of the room. If it were just me in the office tonight, I would've been happy with the setup, satisfied that every single step Michael takes would have been noticed. However, with whatever Ross has up his sleeve on the way, I'm even happier.

I walk down the stairs and use the time to familiarise myself with the building. In the main room, Andy is directing a group of men and women who will be undercover tonight to an area of the club. Wherever Michael goes, someone on our team will be within a few feet of him. I can only hope that the selected officers have glad rags into which they can slip.

Bottles clink behind the bar as someone restocks the fridges, while another polishes the bar's mirrored top. A door to the right of the bar leads to a stock room. A silver plaque at eye level tells the punters that it is to be used by employees only, though one of the team will remain nearby at all times.

A fire escape on the back wall, situated between two of the VIP booths, leads to an alleyway that runs the length of the building, connecting two busy streets. A car park opposite is the designated meeting point in the event of an emergency, though I imagine panic would send inebriated party goers in all directions in the search for safety.

The only other door in the room, aside from the stockroom, fire escape and entrance, is on the opposite wall to the bar. The door leads to a short corridor with marbled floor, walls and ceiling. It's a disorientating cuboid. The only thing to break up the natural stone are two black doors, opposite each other, identical but for the silver cut out of a man on one and a woman on the other.

In the men's toilet, a row of metallic urinals line one wall. Three cubicles run the length of another wall, while a large mirror claims the third. Under the mirror, three sinks complete with mixer taps and fancy hand soap fill the rest of the space. It's minimalistic and in keeping with the rest of the club.

On the other side of the corridor, it's similar, aside from the urinals. In their place are more cubicles. There is also one more sink and lots more hand gel.

Happy that everything is as it should be and that I know the layout of the building, I make my way back towards the main room. The group that Andy had been directing have left and he is sitting at the bar, sipping water through a straw.

'Everyone know what they're doing?' I ask.

He nods.

'There's also been a development. Arabella has just rung in. She wasn't supposed to be working tonight but she's become available.'

'Convenient,' I say.

'A little too convenient,' he replies. 'I propose a wager. I know how strongly you feel about your own suspect, so how about we put a couple of quid on it. You give me a fiver if it's Arabella, and I give you a fiver if it's who you think it is.'

'We're betting on a murderer?' I ask.

He nods and I extend my arm, offering my hand.

'Money in the bank,' he says, as he hops off his stool.

32

SHE LOOKS DOWN at his thinning body and feels a momentary stab of pity. Still, it's his own fault. She's trying to look after him. She gives him food and water and the space she provided for him was ample for exercise.

He looks up at her, though the light flooding through the doorway she is standing in means he only sees a silhouette. She's been vigilant in ensuring that he has never seen her face. He mumbles something, his voice hoarse, though she makes no effort to try and make out what he's saying. Instead, she throws a packet of cigarettes down the stairs. They land with a soft thud on the concrete below. He makes no attempt to get them, though his eyes have wandered towards them.

In a fluid motion, she steps back and closes the door, triple checking that the lock has turned. She walks to the kitchen table and pulls out her phone, checking her social media again, just in case Michael Sims has changed his mind.

He hasn't.

A laugh erupts from her mouth. Three bodies so far and it's been so easy. No one suspects a damn thing. And then, the presenter that Johnny so obviously despises delivers himself like a lamb to the slaughter.

Her plan was almost through. One more body and then she'd hang Johnny out to dry, framing him for the murders which would ensure her freedom.

Of course, she wasn't stupid.

Michael Sims appearance at the night club was fortuitous, yes, but it also set quiet alarm bells off for the first time.

Was it a set up?

She didn't think so. There was no way anyone could know that Michael was on her list. It was simply a coincidence, and a happy one at that.

Still, arrangements had been made. Tonight was the only time she felt like she was taking a risk. A celebrity in a public place was taking things

CHRIS MCDONALD

up a notch and if something were to go wrong, it would be prudent to have a backup plan. Which, she had.

After packing her handbag and checking again on the door leading to the cellar, she makes her way to the living room. She smiles at the large gas canister in the corner of the room. She bends down in front of it and runs a hand over the cold metal, before turning the nozzle. Immediately, butane gas starts to hiss out; a slow stream but enough to fill the room in a few hours. She leaves the living room door open and walks to the kitchen, repeating the process with the blue canister under the table.

She leaves via the back door and walks around to her car, pleased with the plan of action. If everything goes as planned, she can get home and open the windows, let the butane out before staying at a friend's house for a few days while the gas empties. If things go wrong, she trusts Johnny to be the spark in his own downfall.

As she walks towards the car, she catches sight of herself in the wing mirror and smiles. The black dress she has chosen for tonight really shows her at her best. She unlocks the car and slips into the driver's seat, pausing only to pull the dark wig onto her head.

It's show time.

33

ONLY WHEN HE hears the door close above him, does he push himself off the mattress to retrieve the cigarette box. He scrabbles around in the near darkness until his hand makes contact with the cool cardboard. He picks the box up and is disappointed at how light it feels. When he pulls the top off, he's even more disappointed to find that there are only two cigarettes.

He pulls one out immediately and jams it between his lips. He reaches under his bed for the lighter that had been in his pocket when she had brought him here. He holds it to the tip of the cigarette, then stops.

He considers his actions. If he only has two cigarettes to last him for who knows how long, then he needs to be sensible. He should wait until he is really desperate, otherwise it'll feel like a waste. However, the notion of a lungful of smoke is too much, and any sensible thought is pushed out of his brain. He lights the end and sucks it in.

The horror of recent days recedes for a few minutes, as the sweet rush of nicotine courses through his body. When he finishes, he stubs the first out and reaches for the second. He sparks the lighter to life, and then kills it again.

Reluctantly, he pulls the second cigarette from his mouth, and tucks it back inside the box.

He sits down on the mattress and sighs deeply.

'Fuck,' he mutters to no one.

34

TONY, WHO HAS transformed from vampire by day to glamorous club host by night, checks with me one last time that everything is in place and that we are happy to let the great and the good of Manchester enter the club. I look up at Ross Powell, who gives me the nod.

Tony closes the office door behind him and his footsteps sound on the wooden steps as he descends. On the CCTV screens, we watch him enter the main room of the club. All of the staff, aside from Arabella who is not here yet, know about the operation in place for tonight. Tony walks around the room, checking with his employees that they are ready for the club to be open, before walking to the huge, wooden doors and unlocking them.

My heart hammers in my chest as well-dressed, good-looking people make their way slowly up the steps and through the doors. Tony stands at the side, greeting the guests as if he were a priest welcoming his flock. Nearly everyone who passes through the doors hugs him, and Tony looks to be in his element, his wide smile evident through the screens.

Ten minutes later, the bar is crammed with people, arms extended and waving notes in the hope of attracting one of the bar workers, who, despite having smiles plastered on their faces, already look like they've had enough. A man I recognise from one of the Northern soaps leaves the bar clutching a hefty bottle of champagne, with a waist-coated man trailing behind him, carrying a tray of empty glasses. They pick a table at the side, casting envious glances at the empty VIP area they are perhaps not *quite* important enough to enter.

The action picks up and before long the dance floor has its first visitors. A group of women in short dresses and tall heels that make my feet hurt just looking at them dance on the peripheries, not quite brave enough to take centre stage so early on in the evening. A few more drinks and it'll be a different story.

With no sound, it's an odd thing to watch—like a silent movie in high definition. My attention is taken away from the dancing women by Michael Sims and his two friends. They enter and greet Tony with a handshake, before heading to the bar. Michael's taller friend orders the drinks while the presenter reaches under his shirt. Immediately, the deafening buzz of the club fills our little office. Ross reaches over to the speaker's controls and turns the volume down, just as Michael speaks.

'I hope you're getting this,' he says.

We'd made the decision to put a hidden recording device on him, so that we could hear and record any conversations he has. This way, we'll be able to hear anything he says and if he is in trouble, one of the undercover officers nearby can rush to his assistance. We'd also made the decision not to give him an earpiece so that, if our killer does show, they won't be any wiser about the covert operation Michael is part off.

The group of friends walks away from the bar and stand near the back, close to the VIP area, but not entering it. We'd decided that if he did go in there, it may make him seem unattainable. Instead, he loiters anxiously, flinching at anyone who walks past. Already, he is attracting glances, admiring or otherwise. A young man in a paisley shirt shuffles over and begins a conversation, telling Michael how much he enjoyed the documentaries. Michael's voice quivers and he is abrupt in his replies. The young man gets the message quickly, slouching back to his group of mates with a hollow goodbye.

Michael rubs a hand over his face and stalks off to the bar, barging in between thirsty regulars, which earns him some dirty looks he remains oblivious to. He gets served quickly and throws one shot down his neck, and then another.

I radio into one of the undercover team and ask them to relay the message to Michael that he can't have any more to drink. On the screen, I watch Dave nod his head and make his way across the bar area to where the presenter is. He leans in close to Michael, and I can hear Dave impart my missive verbatim. Michael rolls his eyes and, as Dave turns to walk away, he grabs the officer's arm.

'I'm freaking out,' he whispers.

Dave gives him a sympathetic look before reminding him that he is surrounded by trained professionals who couldn't give a fuck about the music, the people or the booze. Everyone is here with two objectives—keeping him safe and catching the killer. Michael puts on a brave face, claps Dave on the shoulder and walks back to his group of friends. Dave returns to his position on the other side of the room.

Just then, a figure of great importance enters via the front doors. Arabella Neale totters in, wearing an impossibly short, figure hugging dress that causes many heads to turn in her direction. She seems oblivious to the staring as she makes her way confidently through the crowd towards the door labelled employees only. When she emerges, she adjusts her dark wig slightly—centring it, before moving behind the bar and collecting a tray of shots. She exits the bar area and works the zone around the dancefloor, hips swaying sexily in an attempt to entice paying customers towards her.

It works well.

The moment she notices Michael Sims, my heart begins to hammer. She stands frozen for a moment, before acting as if nothing has changed, instead lavishing her attention on men with tongues lolling who are waving tenners in her direction.

Though my pulse has quickened, seeing the reaction changes nothing in my mind. Yes, she is someone of interest who has a relationship with two of the victims, but I still feel strongly about my suspect. Still, it's good to see one of the uniformed team tail her as she makes her way around the room.

As the night passes, I wonder if Arabella did notice Michael at all. She certainly hasn't taken any notice of him since, nor tried to interact with him in any way. As I'm pondering this, Ross stirs me from my thoughts.

'Is that her?' he asks, pointing to the bottom row of monitors. On it, a tall, slim woman in a dark dress strides confidently towards the back of the club, giving the dancefloor a wide berth. She pushes past a dancing man who has clearly had too much to drink and leans against the wall near the fire exit door, hidden behind a group of people. From her covert position, she seems to be staring in Michael's direction.

After a few minutes, she sets off again, though her gait is different. It's as if she is feigning drunkenness. Her steps are erratic and she stumbles. Michael's attention is drawn as she almost falls into him. He reaches out and grabs her around the waist to stop her falling to the floor.

'Thank you,' she slurs, her voice picked up through the presenter's hidden microphone. She looks up at him. 'You're Mr Sims, aren't you?'

There is mock surprise in her voice.

'Michael,' he replies, his voice shaking.

'Well, I'm a huge fan,' she says, stroking his chest seductively. 'Can I get you a drink?'

He declines, holding up an almost full pint of beer, the same one he's been holding for the past hour.

'I've had too much already,' she laughs, throwing her head back and allowing us our first unobstructed look at her face.

I was right.

The laughing face belongs to Susie Lyons, ex-wife of Eli Parker and my *friend* from NCT.

'Do you want to come back to my hotel room?' Michael asks, quietly.

'You want to fuck me?'

He nods, though I can tell he doesn't mean it, it's simply part of the plan.

'I can't wait that long,' she says. 'Let's go to the toilets.'

She yanks on his arm, and he allows himself to be dragged after her a for a few steps, though the reluctance to follow her into the toilet clear on his face.

'Delay them,' I shout into the microphone.

I watch as an undercover officer bumbles his way towards the presenter, grabbing him and mumbling faux-drunkenly about how much he loves his interviews as I make my way out of the door and fly down the stairs. I enter the club and make my way across it, deliberately staying out of the area where Michael and Susie are.

I make my way to the toilet door and find Andy and two undercover officers standing in the corridor, clearly having heard the exchange in their earpieces. Andy and one of the officers duck into the men's toilet while Dave and myself enter the women's. We can't know which toilet Susie will choose.

The toilet is empty. We enter separate cubicles and wait. Through the crack in the door, I have a view of the length of the tiled room. A minute later, the door pushes open and Susie enters, followed by a harried looking Michael. I realise that he must feel abandoned, having no way of knowing that help is so close at hand. Susie lets Michael walk past her and then turns the lock on the door, sealing them in.

'Which cubicle do you fancy?' he asks, his voice high.

He is met with a mirthless laugh.

'You stupid, stupid man,' Susie says. 'I don't want to have sex with you. You were the last past of the puzzle and you presented yourself like a gift-wrapped present. You see, I'm going to kill you and frame Johnny Mayhem. He must hate you after how you showed him on your shitty little documentary.'

'You've killed the others? Michael whimpers.

'Keep up,' she says, as she takes a kitchen knife from her handbag, the bright spotlights glinting on the metallic blade. 'It really is nothing personal.'

I knock twice on the door of the cubicle before Dave and I burst out of our hiding places at the same time. Dave is closest to Michael and runs to him, rugby tackling him to the floor at the same time Susie hurls the knife in his direction. Had Dave not taken such action, the metal blade would be embedded in the presenter's stomach. As it is, it clatters off the back wall and bounces harmlessly on to the tiled floor before coming to rest.

As Susie's throwing arm falls back to her side, I tackle her to the ground. Her shoulder collides roughly with the sink, knocking it off the wall and onto the floor, where it explodes into hundreds of sharp pieces. Water erupts from the exposed pipe.

Susie is momentarily disorientated and I manage to scrabble on top of her. I grab her arms and pin them to the floor, though her knees slam into my back and the bucking of her hips is causing me to fall forward. She aims a headbutt at me, but I manage to avoid it.

As I'm about to lose my grip on her arms, the door is kicked open—the wooden frame collapsing under the weight of the boot—and Andy runs in. He and Dave bring Susie's flailing limbs under control as I slip the cuffs around her skinny wrists and place her under arrest.

We pull her up and lead her out of the fire escape towards the waiting police car. Once she is safely detained in the back seat, the officer drives her away towards the police station, a small cell awaiting her. Before following the car to begin the questioning, I return to the club. Michael is still hunkered in the corner of the woman's toilet, being talked to gently by Dave.

Surrounded by the smashed ceramic, puddles of water and the destroyed door frame, he looks like a stricken soldier in a very strange, nicely scented war. His eyes are wide and he is nodding at whatever Dave is saying, though he doesn't look like he's taking any of it in. Dave and I pick him up under the armpits and force him into a standing position. We lead him to another police car and he gets in. Dave gets behind the steering wheel with instructions to take Michael to the hospital for a once over.

I knock on the window and Michael looks at me with faraway eyes.

'We couldn't have done it without you,' I say, before banging the top of the car and watching it disappear into the night.

35

THE ATMOSPHERE IN the small interview room is strange. Susie sits on the other side of the table, looking completely out of place with a full face of make-up and wearing her little black dress. Her blonde hair shines under the strip light on the low ceiling, her brunette wig discarded. She looks deflated, knowing the plan she'd had in her head all along has now come to an unsatisfactory and incriminating end. Her shoulders are stooped as if the weight of the world has been hoisted onto them in the past hour. Her eyes are downcast, refusing to meet mine.

Beside her is a court appointed lawyer, here because Susie refused to call her own. The sleep is still fresh in his eyes. A tuft of hair on the left side of his head sticks up at an unnatural angle and the creases in his shirt show that he got dressed in a hurry, and possibly in the dark. He takes off his glasses and wipes them with his stripy tie, before replacing them and fixing us with a sleepy stare.

I press a button on the recorder and begin my spiel.

'Interview with Susan Lyons commencing at 3.23 a.m. Present are Detective Inspector Erika Piper, Detective Sergeant Andy Robinson and Mr Stephen Holley, Miss Lyons's appointed lawyer.'

I fix my eyes on the top of Susie's head before addressing her. It feels oddly formal questioning someone who, before tonight, I'd considered a friend. To think that this woman had been in my house and had offered to babysit Leo while she'd also been murdering people in the area is chilling.

'Miss Lyons, this is simply a formality, as we have a voice recording of you admitting to three counts of murder and evidence of you attempting to kill again. I simply want your side of the story.'

She looks up at me and for a moment, I expect to see something in her eyes. A softness, maybe? A silent plea for forgiveness. What I'm met with is different. There's a challenge etched in her dark pupils.

'I know what I did and you know what I did. What I want to know is, how did you figure it out. I'll tell you if you're close.'

'Okay, here goes. With Duane, we were at a loss. It looked for all the world that Mayhem was behind it. With Simon, that's where the case started to turn. The hairs left behind from your wig reminded me of the Amanda Mayhem crime scene. There was a synthetic hair discovered there too. No one thought much of it at the time. The case was open and shut—everyone, including myself, though Johnny was behind it. But the hair was noted in the log and it stood out to me when I was revising it. At that stage, I simply though Johnny was wearing a wig to avoid detection. Killing Eli was a risky one. You must've known your name would come up, being his first wife and all. But, when we came to break the news to you, you played us well. Even then I didn't suspect you.'

'So, what changed?'

'A call to a florist.'

Her expression changes to one of genuine intrigue.

'When you sent the flowers to me, in an effort to make it look like a threat from Johnny, you gave yourself away. Firstly, there's no way anyone else connected to the case could've known where I live. Delivering them in the dead of night was your first mistake. Your second was what was inside the envelope. The lavender rose is a symbol of enchantment and love at first sight. The florist also told me it's often associated with royalty. Johnny often called Amanda his queen, and when we found her body, he'd put the lavender rose in her hand. A goodbye to his queen. He would never have sent me it as a threat, now laid it in the hand of anyone he'd killed.

After that, I went back over the case. The open condom wrapper at Duane's suggested that it was a woman who had killed him. His friend balked when I suggested that Duane may have had homosexual feelings. It would have been easy for you to suggest sex to him at the club to get into his bedroom. Same with Simon. I'd mentioned his name once to you. From there, it was easy to find him at his new place of work. You got chatting, booked some building work, found out he was on a dating site and masqueraded as Becky. You don't make it to the bar, but do manage to show up at his house and club him to death. How am I doing so far?'

'Quite well,' she answers, a vague suggestion of a smile on her glossy lips.

'Eli was easy. He was a cheater then and a cheater now and you knew he would come running. You knew about Amanda and him all those years ago. It was you who took the photos and it was you who killed Amanda.'

She nods.

'I went round to her house. Eli had left the address lying about so I went round to warn her off. The door was lying open and when I went in, she was lying on the bed, in sexy lingerie waiting for my husband to fuck her. I grabbed a baseball bat and hit her. I didn't mean to kill her, but it happened. When Johnny got arrested, I was delighted. Until he was put in jail, I hardly slept. I was worried he'd find some sort of way out, but he never did and I could breathe easy again. Then, he gets released and you told me yourself that the case would be reopened.'

'So, you planned to frame Johnny for these killings?'

'You said yourself that he was released on flimsy evidence. I thought that if I killed people he'd have bad feelings towards, they'd come for him again and I wouldn't have to worry. When I released him into the wild again, he'd have no idea where he'd been and the police would've had an easy arrest.'

'You're a disgrace. What about your son?'

'I never fucking wanted him,' she shouts. 'I got pregnant from a one-night stand with a guy I fucking detest. I couldn't give a fuck about Adam.'

My anger rises and I stand, throwing my chair back and letting it ricochet of the wall. My own pregnancy woes flash through my head and bile rises in my throat at Susie's admission. Andy picks up the chair behind me as I continue to stare at Susie with flames dancing in my eyes. Before I can say anything, Andy speaks.

'Where is Johnny?'

She taps her nose and winks at him.

'Is he safe?' I ask.

'That depends on how desperate he is for a ciggie. He may be alive and well, or, he could be a smoking corpse.'

Flashes of being in her living room come back to me. The Night Nurse on her sideboard and her "out of order" downstairs toilet.

'You've been drugging him, haven't you? Feeding him sleeping medicine and then putting his prints all over the murder weapons?'

She nods.

I turn to Andy.

'I know where he is.'

We run out of the interview room and instruct Angela to make sure Susie is escorted safely to a cell, before making our way down the stairs towards a car. I pull my phone out and dial the fire station in Marple.

'Reg here,' a gruff voice answers.

'It's Erika Piper,' I shout as I throw myself into the passenger side of the car as Andy fires up the engine. 'You need to get over to Hazeldene Farm. I think something big is going to happen.'

36

JOHNNY AWOKE WITH a start.

He'd been having that nightmare again, with Amanda's warm embrace just out of reach. He sat up, coughing and ran a hand over his heavy eyes. His heart was hammering so hard that he imagined it was painting bloody patterns against his ribs.

Through the small section of window, he watches the stars twinkle in the inky sky, lamenting the choices that had led him here, to this basement, with his unknown tormentor and keeper.

Turning his back on the darkness outside, he feels his way back to the mattress where he sits down heavily. He stretches out a hand, feeling for the cardboard packet in the gloom. Finally, his fingers curl around the packet and he opens the lid, extracting the solitary cigarette that is left and the lighter. With a sigh, he places it between his chapped lips where it sticks like a plaster. He takes it out again and tries to summon some saliva, wiping his now damp tongue over his lips. He reinserts the cigarette and holds the lighter to it.

A swirl of blue light flashes through the window.

His already rushing heartbeat rises further.

Could rescue be on its way? Could he be about to be saved?

The regularity of the flashing and the roar of a nearby engine cause him to stand and look out the window. He can see shapes in the distance, getting closer.

A smile spreads across his face. The first smile that has broken across his features in an age. His facial muscles protest at the sudden workout.

Without thinking, he lifts the lighter to his lips again and rolls his thumb along the metal wheel, causing a spark to briefly flicker before the house explodes around him.

37

THE DARK NIGHT suddenly lights up, as if a thousand suns have sprung to life. Flames erupt through the roof of the farmhouse as the front wall explodes outwards, causing bricks to rain down on the parked emergency vehicles, making the fire fighters run for cover. Thick black clouds of smoke billow out of the destroyed house, creeping eerily through the air, making it unbreathable.

When the debris has settled on the ground, the firefighters emerge from their vehicles, shouting instructions to each other. Some run to the back of the fire engine and begin unfurling the hoses, unwinding them as far as they can go. Thick plumes of smoke envelop the area around us, reducing visibility to almost zero. The shouts of the firefighters get louder, battling over the sounds of the house's destruction. Suddenly, the hoses leap to life and the whoosh of pressurised water joins the crackling of the flames as the battle to get the situation under control begins in earnest.

I feel helpless, watching it happen and knowing that I can't do anything to help. The urge to run in and find Johnny Mayhem is almost overwhelming, though at this stage it looks like forensics will be removing a charred corpse instead.

Within ten minutes, the worst of the flames have been brought under control and a plan to search the house is quickly put together. Firefighters don protective masks and walk carefully towards the remains of the building. The dying flames and burning embers are still being soaked by jets of water, but a path has been opened up for the rescuers to follow. High powered spotlights cast a bright glow on the front of the house and torches attached to the fronts of uniforms will lead the rescuers into the bowels of the house untouched by the light.

The walls have long since crumbled leaving only foundation boundaries, like those seen in long extinct towns like Pompeii.

Minutes pass that feel like hours, each second a ticking time bomb that threatens to snuff out Johnny Mayhem's life, if it hasn't already. Crackling on the radios of the firefighters who have remained to battle the last of the flames give a running commentary of the search. No sign of life. So far.

I pace around the garden, keeping my eyes firmly on the house, despite the heat threatening to singe my retinas and the ash that falls around us like darkened snowflakes. My attention is drawn to the firefighters. Their body language has changed, despite no official confirmation from inside. They think it's a lost cause. The paramedics stand by, waiting to perform a miracle.

Time is the enemy.

So too, is the silence that surrounds us.

A distorted crackle from the radio of the fire fighter next to me makes me jump. I struggle to make out what has been said, though whatever it is pushes the crew into action. The paramedics spring forward, getting as close to the house as possible with equipment at the ready.

In the shadows of the house, a silhouette emerges, growing larger and more solid until it becomes obvious what it is.

Two of the firefighters emerge, carrying a body. They walk slowly over the uneven ground that is littered with rubble, careful not to take a tumble. When clear of the dangers, they set the damaged body onto the stretcher that has been brought forward by the paramedics.

Through the mass of emergency workers, I get my first glimpse of Johnny's body. Vicious red welts cover his blackened torso. A section of his hair has been burned away, leaving a raw scalp in its place.

A tube is carefully inserted into his mouth before being passed into his throat.

His chest is still.

Unmoving.

As one paramedic works on his airways, another prepares the defibrillator, pressing a few buttons on the machine. He raises the pads and places them on Johnny's bare chest, before shouting clear. Johnny's body bucks as an electric current passes through it. The paramedic observes for a moment, before delivering another shock that ends with the same outcome.

I can only observe as the treatment continues. The shit that Johnny has had to put up with flashes before me.

His cheating wife was murdered and he got the blame.

He paid the price for that—seven undeserved years in prison, with the knowledge that his wife's killer was roaming free.

Upon his release, he was taken prisoner in the home of his wife's killer while she orchestrated murders with the goal of framing him again.

The unfairness of it all is staggering and I find myself willing him to take a breath. To not let Susie win. I plead with a god that hasn't answered me before.

Just one breath.

And then, he does.

His chest rises slightly and his mouth opens, sucking in a lungful of not altogether clean air. It causes him to cough and splutter. His hands claw at the tubes that pump life into him, though the paramedics quickly sedate him.

As his body relaxes and his eyes begin to close, they lock with mine. His silent gratitude collides with my soundless apologies.

Seven years' worth of them.

His eyes close and, with that, it's all over.

EPILOGUE

Five months later

THE BLINDING LIGHTS blink in time with the pounding bassline and as the song reaches it frenetic conclusion, the arena fills with darkness. A solitary spotlight flickers on and illuminates the singer of the popular indie rock band. He pushes long, sweaty hair out of his eyes and raises his fist in the air.

'Fuck Susie Lyons,' he says, to a roar of approval, before striding off the stage and into the embrace of his bandmates who were waiting in the wings. The house lights come on as the intermission begins, allowing those thirsty enough to brave the queue to do so.

'You fancy another?' Tom asks, holding up his empty cup.

'Go on, then,' I reply.

He eases past me and I watch him as he makes his way slowly up the concrete steps towards the concourse. When he is out of sight, I turn my attention back to the expanse of the arena. The atmosphere is electric—the Johnny Mayhem benefit was planned to coincide with the day of Susie's sentencing. The mood inside the arena is celebratory as she got exactly what she deserved. Despite no band being on stage, a sing-a-long has started in the pit area, though all three sides of the venue quickly join in as it reaches the rousing chorus.

Hearing the words that Johnny wrote all those years ago in tribute to his then living wife, sang a cappella by an arena full of strangers, brings a tear to my eye. I wipe it away just as Tom returns and hands me my beer.

'Just heard from mum,' he says, sitting down. 'Leo is out for the count.'

He takes a swig from his plastic cup and rubs his free hand over my knee. His stance on my work had softened in the preceding months, after the conclusion of the Mayhem case, and seeing the joy on my face earlier when Susie's sentence was handed down had changed something in him. He'd sort of mumbled something about me doing a good job, which I took as his blessing for me to continue.

The lights go down again amid oohs and aahs from the crowd. A video begins on the curtain that has been erected to block the stage, showing The Darling Roses in their pomp—fresh faced and newly blooded. Halfway through the accompanying song that is blaring from the PA system, the images fade, leaving the white material bare.

The music fades away too.

The room is silent in anticipation.

Behind the curtain, a silhouette forms. It stands tall and proud before another joins it on the other side of the stage. The cheering from the crowd is ear splitting—everyone knows what's going to happen next and the place is at fever pitch.

The curtain drops to expose the four figures.

The Darling Roses, minus Johnny Mayhem.

They launch into a fast paced rock song. The bass and drums become intertwined, forming a solid base for Glenn Lumb's thrashy guitar riff. His smile is wide as he surveys the sold-out arena crowd. He strikes the typical rock star moves as he stalks across the stage, making sure everyone who wants a piece of him gets it.

And then, the noise swells again.

Emerging from the curtain at the side of the stage, Johnny Mayhem takes unsteady steps across the boards towards the microphone. When he gets there, he stands like a statue and looks out at the crowd. His face fills the huge screens on either side of the stage and the emotion is clear to see. Tears stream down his face and his chin quivers.

The rest of the musicians stop playing, except for the bassist who fills the arena with a low, steady, single-note rumble. Johnny nods his appreciation once at his disciples, before stretching both arms out wide as the guitar and drums kick in again, this time complete with Johnny's vocals. Glenn strolls over and the two of them stand back to back, savouring a moment neither of them thought they'd ever have again.

ACKNOWLEDGEMENTS

This was an emotional book to finish, as it marks the end of the Erika Piper series. I'd like to say thank you to a number of people.

Firstly, Thank YOU for reading my book. I have been absolutely blown away by the love and support that the series and myself have received. I thought I'd write one, and that'd be enough – that no one would care as much about Erika as I did. How wrong I was. Thanks for coming on a journey with her and I, and for all the kind words along the way.

Hopefully you'll stick around for what is coming next…

Sean at Red Dog Press is a machine. Editor, sounding board, friend and the best cover designer in the game. Without him, I'd be nowhere and I owe him the world.

To all the authors who have accepted me as one of their own. I've considered giving up on more than one occasion, but the friendships I've made with other writers keeps me hanging in there!

Funeral For A Friend are one of my favourite bands, and Roses For The Dead is one of their songs. I got in touch with Matt, their singer, who very kindly granted me permission to use it as the title for the book. Fifteen year old me was stoked at even getting an answer.

To my Blood Brothers—Sean Coleman (again) and Rob Parker. I continue to find myself inspired weekly by the authors who come on our show. If it weren't for you two, I wouldn't be in this position. Thank you for the laughs, the inspiration and the sheer craziness that the pod has brought along with it (namely, organising a festival!)

To everyone on Twitter—old friends and new, you've kept me going this year during a very strange time. Big shout out to Kon Frankowski, Steven Kedie, JD Whitelaw and the Cheese Wheel of Trust (or whatever it is called now) for checking in and keeping me going at times. You'll never know how much it's meant.

Here's to the future and actually seeing each other in the flesh!

On behalf of Erika and myself, goodbye!